The Island

Dan Padavona

Other Books by Dan Padavona

Storberry

Shadow Witch

Dark Vanishings 1-4

Published by Dan Padavona

Visit our website at www.danpadavona.com

The Island

The Island

The Island

The Little Princess exploded at high noon.

Ben's eyes searched for his son as he ducked his head underwater to avoid the bits of yacht shrapnel raining down around him. His eyes opened to a sea of turquoise, schools of fish darting across the ocean floor like the shadow of migrating birds.

A million thoughts raced through his mind—sharks, the pull of the tide, ocean depth, his missing son. His eyes centered on a conglomeration of coral, beautiful yet sharp as knives. Coughing out the choking sea, he thrust his head out of the water, kicking his legs and spinning in a circle.

"Matt!"

A gray plume rose from the remnants of the yacht, bending over horizontally about a hundred yards off the ocean surface as it caught stronger winds above the water. *Are we close enough to St. Kitts for someone to see the smoke?* The smell of diesel was on the wind, mixing with sea salt and acrid smoke.

"Dad! Over here!"

Ben spun 180-degrees to see Matt swimming in his direction. At sixteen, Matt was already a much stronger swimmer than his father. He glided through the water, closing the distance between them.

"Slow down, Matt. Look out for reefs."

Matt reached Ben, and they held onto each other, bobbing in the water like buoys.

"What did you say?"

"I said you need to look out for coral. It's everywhere underneath us."

Matt pointed toward a hill of lush greens and black rock jutting out of the sea in front of them and asked, "What island is that?"

"Don't know. But we had better get to it quick. Just

keep an eye out for coral."

The island, no more than a hundred yards long and wide, had the appearance of a humpbacked, slumbering dinosaur. Ben and Matt swam more cautiously toward the island, putting distance between themselves and the burning remains of their sinking yacht. Reaching the shallows, they walked through gentle waves which lowered from chest-deep to thigh-high over several steps.

As Matt smiled at his father, Ben saw the doubt in his eyes. Ben wondered, *where are we, and how in the hell are we going to get back to civilization?*

"How far do you think we are from the resort?" Matt asked.

"Can't be too far."

"We lost track of the shore over an hour ago."

Ben didn't know what he could say that would allay his son's fear. Truth be told, he had the same concern. They could be ten or fifteen miles from civilization; and once the smoke plume dissipated, there would be no trace of their existence.

They emerged from the water amid gentle breakers onto a white sand shoreline choked with an overgrowth of palm trees. Something sharp and hard crawled over Ben's foot, and he jumped. A crab the size of a fist lumbered toward the water.

"At least we won't have trouble finding food," Ben said, watching the crab submerge. "We should stay out of the sun while we figure out what we are going to do."

Like a wet sponge, the July air encased the island in smothering humidity. It was no cooler under the shadows of the palms, but at least they were out of the sun. Something rustled the leaves overhead, and Matt ducked as a white-tailed hawk plunged out of a palm as though it was an arrow shot from a bow. The hawk whistled over their heads and veered toward the shore where it swooped into the shallows, emerging with a fish wiggling in its talons.

5

"Better him than us," Ben said with a forced laugh.

Beyond the palms drifted crystal waters, stretching endlessly toward the horizon. The main islands of the Lesser Antilles couldn't be more than a dozen miles away but in which direction? Palm fronds rustled like distant laughter, the leaves put into motion by a thickening ocean breeze.

"How are we going to—"

"We'll find a way. I promise."

Ben pulled off his shoes and socks, leaving them in the sun to dry. Matt sat down and copied his father.

Behind them, the palms joined with lush ferns and a sea of green vegetation, rising in humps toward the island center. The terrain surface, charcoal-black and loamy, was visible only in scattered patches where the green did not smother the land completely.

In the movies, Ben thought, the stranded saved themselves by spelling out a distress signal on the shore. He wondered if in the world's history this methodology had ever worked outside of a Hollywood movie set. Still, he had to try something. He peered up into the rising jungle, its interior shadowed and forbidding. Cold reality began to dawn on him. The day had been ethereal—the idyllic beauty of the crystal seas, the explosion, and now this lunatic Robinson Crusoe scenario. It seemed as though he were walking in a dream, waiting for his wife to shake him awake. Incredibly, he was stranded on an unknown island with Matt, with no idea how to get back to civilization.

"Let's gather as much wood and dry brush as we can find," Ben said. "A lot of the wood might be damp, so the sooner we can drag it into the sun to dry, the better."

"You think we're going to be here for a while, don't you?"

Athletic, and almost as tall as his father, Matt seemed as though he had become an adult overnight; but now he had a look of anxiety in his eyes that reminded Ben that his son was still a boy.

"Somebody will find us, Matt. It's not like we are hundreds of miles from shore. But we need to give ourselves every advantage that we can. That means making a fire, putting out distress signals, gathering rainwater, and finding food. If we stay calm, we'll get out of this. Besides, when we don't return for supper, your mother will have half the world searching for us."

Ben thought about Marie, probably slick with tanning lotion and redolent of coconut oil on the white sand beach of St. Kitts. There would be a band playing, the musical tin of calypso drums filling the air as children splashed in the breakers. They should all be there now—Marie ogling the cabana boy who brought them lunchtime sandwiches, saving her desire for Ben that evening.

Instead he had taken the yacht too far offshore and lost track of the land when the navigation equipment oddly failed. After an hour of drifting without sight of civilization, eyeing the fuel gauge needle which pointed toward one-third of a tank remaining, he had panicked and plunged the yacht toward the island—the first land he'd seen in what seemed an eternity. In his haste he had not seen the rocks ahead of the shallows, and he had rammed the Little Princess into a black mass of boulder just below the ocean surface. The stench of diesel fuel became overwhelming, and as Matt rushed to secure the wheel, Ben heard the wicked crackle of flames from below. Ben had just enough time to pull his son from the wheel and dive into the water before—

"Is it safe to go in there?" Matt asked, staring into the mass of palms which curled over at their tops like talons. Shadows spilled out toward them, massing at the jungle entry.

"Think of the stories you will be able to tell everyone when you get back home, how you braved the jungle."

Matt smiled uneasily and said, "There aren't any...

animals or anything in there, right?"

"Unless Noah dropped them off on a side trip, I highly doubt it." But as Ben looked into the gloom, he heard something rustle in the undergrowth—probably just a bird, or the wind—and began to wonder if a tiger, lion, or even a dinosaur might be hunkered down within the darkness.

"But there could be snakes and stuff, right?"

"Maybe," he said, not sure what types of reptiles inhabited the Lesser Antiles. He had seen his fair share of geckos, and those quick darting anoles that carnivals and pet stores always mistakenly labeled as chameleons. But he had no idea if poisonous snakes made their homes here. "Watch where you step, okay? Take it nice and slow."

Ben led the way, Matt pressed close to him. Ben could feel the flora close behind him, as though a one-way gate swung shut. After climbing the slope for a few minutes, he noticed that everything looked the same. Ferns with fronds that were almost as long as he was tall, stems as thick as a stout light post. He felt Matt's fingers grabbing at the back of his t-shirt, the boy's feet slipping in the soggy loam.

There was slim quantity of fallen wood to be had, and much of what they found was unusable. Matt bent to pick up a thick branch, and the punky wood crumbled in his hand like wet sand. The boy jumped back as a thousand insects neither could identify scrambled out of the wood and into the underbrush. Black beetles, almost metallic looking, with bodies as large as a good-sized cockroach. Shelled bugs that rolled into balls, like the pill bugs Ben played with as a kid, but these bugs were bigger than peanut shells. Centipede-like things that scurried as fast as a hornet could fly.

"That's odd," Ben said.

"What?"

"Those are the first bugs I have seen. You would think we would have a seen a ton more by now. We're in the tropics, after all."

Then, about fifty feet up the slope among the tree tops, the glint of sun, and something glistening caught Ben's eye. It was almost imperceptible within the dancing rays of the sun over the jungle canopy. As he stared, the wind caught the palm fronds and sent the glistening threads into motion. Ben looked upon a spider's web unlike any he had ever seen before. It canvassed the tops of three palms, stretching over the jungle canopy like a safety net.

"What do you see?"

Ben gave a start, his transfixed stare broken by Matt's voice. "Nothing. Let's keep moving."

As he considered the number of spiders required to weave such a web, Ben shivered despite the stifling warmth.

Widely scattered hardwoods grew amid the army of green. The hardwoods that survived were smothered by moss and lichen, as though under attack by the jungle. Parasitic plants took root in the bark, growing horizontally until they turned upward into the diffused light under the canopy.

It was under these trees that they found recently fallen branches dry enough for burning. Each gripping several branches under their arms, Ben led the way back down the slope. As they retraced their path through bent ferns, the vile stickiness of the jungle interior clung to their skin like a wet suit. Something indiscernible and disturbing also pressed upon them, as though the jungle might spring to life and consume them.

When they exited the jungle, sweat pouring off their bodies, Ben felt a strange disquiet as though he had passed through a graveyard. The unrelenting sun felt cleansing as the breeze thickened off the water.

Unlike in the movies, the white sand shore was compressed to no more than ten or fifteen yards before the jungle took over. There was just enough room to lay down a dozen pieces of wood and spell out a miniaturized S-O-S.

Ben wondered about the tide. The gentle waves stopped within a few feet of the wood. A slight change in the tide would yank the wood into the sea where it would perish with the smoldering remnants of Little Princess.

Ben squinted into the sun. Neither of them had a watch, but based on the sun's position he reasoned that it was almost two o'clock.

"Let's see how far we can walk around this island. Maybe we can find something that we can use to build a shelter."

"Or maybe we will see land from the other side of the island," Matt said with renewed optimism in his eyes. Ben nodded in agreement, not expecting to see anything except an endless ocean.

The sand was hot in the blazing sunshine, and they took to walking through the shallows to cool their feet. Seashells dug into the soles of their feet, sometimes crumbling beneath them like broken glass. Shadows skittered and darted through the water as schools of fish and crabs wandered closer and retreated.

"If we sharpen a few sticks, do you think we can catch those fish?"

"Now you're thinking," Ben said, ruffling his son's hair. "Matt, we are going to eat like kings. We have an ocean full of fish. And if we can't catch them, we'll just have to settle for crab for dinner. Now all we need to find is a french fry tree." Matt laughed. "Seriously. We'll be fine as long as we have shelter. We can't be far from the islands. Someone will find us even if we have to rough it for a few days."

As they circled the humpbacked island, nothing seemed to change but the position of the sun on their shoulders. Palms and ferns grew up the terrain toward the island center from all points along the shore. More hawks dive-bombed the shallows, snatching fish out of the water. They peered longingly across the rolling waters, searching for signs of land but finding only desolate seas.

A quarter of the way around the island, Ben stopped in his tracks.

A boat.

Matt had been looking across the water and nearly walked into Ben. When he glanced up, he turned his eyes to his father. They looked again at the boat, unbelieving, as though they had found a glistening mirage of water in the middle of an endless desert. Then Matt grinned, and they darted toward the boat, shouting as they ran.

"Hello!"

"Is anyone there?"

"Help!"

"We're stranded!"

The craft, a small motorboat, rocked to the tempo of the rhythmic waves. A thick, weathered rope tied the bow to the base of a palm bent over the waterline. By the look of the rope—barely frayed in the middle and tightly coiled over the majority of its length—Ben figured the boat had been here at least a few weeks but probably not much longer than that. A few inches of standing water covered the motorboat's floor, evidence of passing thunderstorms. Bird guano covered the hull as though the boater had been attacked by pirates armed with paint guns.

He cupped his hands around his mouth and called into the jungle. Matt yelled out, too, turning in a circle as though he expected to find a tourist in a bucket hat wading toward them out of the shallows. They continued for a few minutes, the sensation that something was wrong beginning to eat at Ben.

"Whoever was here, they are long gone. This boat hasn't been driven in at least a week or two," Ben said, pointing to the rainwater inside the boat.

"I wonder if he got lost like we did."

Ben stuck his head inside the boat and saw the fuel gauge needle was a shade above the "E".

"Or ran out of fuel. Seeing this boat is good news, though. That confirms what I said about us being close to civilization. It's not just a coincidence that two boats got lost and found the same island."

"Do you think the person might still be here? Maybe he found shelter up the hill."

Ben grimaced. The last thing he wanted to do was climb up through that jungle again. Leaves rippled and swayed in the breeze, almost as if the jungle was taunting him. On cue with the laughing wind, a cauliflower tower of cumulus rose above the water several miles offshore. Its sides were crisp and white in the afternoon sunshine, appearing as a distant bomb blast. Already the underside of the cloud had grown black, as though night congregated there.

"Speaking of shelter, we had better figure out what we are going to do if it rains. We don't want to be caught in the open in a lightning storm."

Ben led Matt back into the overgrowth, pushing against the thick leaves and stalks to clear a path. The cloud continued to grow over the ocean; and as it rose to cloak the sun, Matt felt a cool shadow sweep down across his neck. He turned his head back to the shore as he walked, longingly watching the motorboat become smaller and smaller, until the jungle wrapped itself around him like a door slamming shut.

"Dad?"

"Yeah?"

"Whose boat do you think that is?"

"I don't know. Could be a fisherman, an islander, or even a sightseer like us."

"If he was stranded on the island, where is he now?"

Ben didn't want to say what was really on his mind, that the guy was dead somewhere in the jungle, his body crawling with those black beetles. He pressed onward, racing against the building storm to find shelter.

12

Matt wrinkled his nose. The air inside the jungle was stagnant, the scent of chlorophyll overwhelming. There was another smell here, too: a smell of death. As he climbed the slope, the damp, black humus under his feet kept slipping out from under him. He fell forward once, caught by a huge cup of fronds that made him look as though he were a pearl trapped inside a giant clam. Ben pulled him up, and Matt looked sheepishly back at the massive fronds, as though thinking they might grow fangs and swallow him whole the next time he made a mistake.

A quarter of the way up the slope, Matt's eye caught a glimpse of light, strangely heliographing in the dappled sunlight. The light seemed to come from nowhere and from everywhere. It glistened white, yellow, and orange in thin strands, bouncing between two towering palms. Ben saw it, too, and shivered, realizing the illusion was caused by a humongous spiderweb spanning at least twenty yards. Then, just before the overgrowth blocked his vision, he thought he saw something football-shaped hanging between the trees, suspended by invisible tethers like a magician's trick. He told himself that it was just a piece of bark from the palms, broken off by the wind and stranded in the webbing; but it sure looked like the dessicated remains of one of those hawks they kept seeing. But that was ridiculous. A spider couldn't kill a hawk. *Could it?*

Matt pressed closer to his father. Ben could no longer tell any portion of the jungle apart from any other. In all directions was a sickly, green version of one of Grimm's haunted forests. There were no pathways, only masses of thick stems, huge leaves, and blackness ahead. Sometimes they brushed against a stout stem, and water pooled within the fronds rained down on them. The water always felt slimy, as though it had coagulated with the jungle.

A thin vine appeared this far up the slope, snaking around fronds and stalks. Ben wondered again about the dangers of poisonous snakes on an isolated island. It seemed unlikely, but in the foreboding darkness of the island jungle anything seemed possible. He began to look up with trepidation and step more carefully.

He heard Matt breathing heavily, almost wheezing. The boy ran track and played basketball, but the suffocating humidity was taking its toll on him.

"Hey, let's slow down a bit," Ben said, again ruffling Matt's hair, which felt like a wet mop in his hand. Matt bent over, hands on knees. His breathing didn't sound right, almost asthmatic. "Maybe we should turn around and get back to the fresh air."

"No," Matt said, hitching between breaths. "I'm fine. We gotta find shelter, right?"

"Yeah, but we're walking around blind. Tell you what, let's cut a diagonal back to the right of where we started. We'll cover more territory, and if worst comes to worst, we'll hit shore."

As they turned to leave, something scurried across the jungle floor several yards away. It was large enough to shake stems and cause an impromptu shower from the upper leaves of the canopy.

"What was that?" Matt watched the blackness into which the thing had crawled.

"Dunno. It was big, though. Probably a rat."

"That wasn't a rat. Besides, how would a rat get onto an island in the middle of the ocean?"

"Are you kidding? Those damn things are everywhere."

But Ben kept watching the gloom, too, chewing on his lip. His body tensed. He felt the urge to pull Matt back from the jungle. *Jesus, I hope it was just a rat.*

Thunder rumbled like a bowling ball rolling along a sky-length alley. They were running out of time.

Ben pulled Matt behind him and began to cut diagonally downslope. The way down was faster, almost too fast. The loose soil kept giving way. Ben and Matt each grabbed stalks and palm trunks to catch themselves. The sky, now a milky white overhead, began to reveal itself through the dense canopy as they descended the slope. The wind started picking up, a salty breeze that snaked its way through the fronds and cooled their skin. Ben could not take comfort in the breeze, for he knew it foretold of stormy weather, and they were still without shelter.

He strained to keep from screaming, panic locked behind his throat, fearing his son would see the terror on his face. Here he was: trapped on an unknown island off the Lesser Antilles, preparing to die of a lightning strike that could just as easily kill him on Cape Cod or in some burg in Nebraska.

A silent tension hung in the air, like a coiled spring, and he thought he smelled ozone. Lightning ripped across the sky, fiery fingers tearing a hole through building gray. He was counting the seconds in his head, remembering that a five second delay between lightning and thunder meant the strike was a mile away. Thunder rumbled before he reached four, rolling through the ground as though a volcano was about to erupt.

The panic started pushing past Ben's throat now, rushing outward like a rancid, roiling vapor that was sure to destroy Matt's confidence in him. The wind became a force, ripping leaves and sending the jungle into a frenzied dance. He felt his hair stand on end, and as he turned to yell for Matt to hit the ground, a blinding bolt of lightning struck the shore, followed immediately by an explosion of thunder that shook palms and caused the ground to buckle.

As Ben and Matt ducked under a pair of palms, the wind parted the leaves to reveal something different just ahead of their path. It appeared dark and depthless, as though a small portion of night had broken from the sky and fallen to this permanent jungle prison, where it lay stranded under the unrelenting sun. Ben could see Matt squinting his eyes, staring toward the unknown source of darkness.

Without thinking, Ben grabbed Matt by the elbow and rushed forward.

Thunder pealed through the jungle, and Ben could feel, rather than see the lightning that spoked between two black clouds spinning over the island. The dark hole drew nearer, and then it took form—a cave. As their eyes met, Ben had a wide grin on his face. How could he have been so lucky? He had found the perfect shelter hidden in the almost impenetrable jungle. Without another word, they sprinted toward the cave as the first huge, tropical raindrops splattered down on them.

They saw none of the rocks one might expect outside the entrance to a cave. In fact, as they ducked inside the five-foot wide circular entrance, it seemed more a tunnel than a cave, as though a Jurassic era worm had burrowed into the side of the loamy hill. The light fell away a few yards ahead, and Ben realized uneasily that any sort of animal could be inside the tunnel just beyond their view. An animal with razors for claws and jaws that could bite through a leg bone. That was crazy, of course. There were no dangerous animals on these islands. But as he rested his back against the earthen sides of the tunnel, his eyes kept wandering toward the edge of darkness, a prickling fear running up his legs.

Rain poured in torrents across the tunnel opening, giving Ben the impression of standing behind a waterfall. The water roared as it cascaded over the tunnel, a vertical stream choked with bits of plant and clumps of black, runny earth.

"Good thing we found this cave. We almost got stuck in that," Ben said, pointing to the deluge.

Matt eyes watched the unmoving black as he said, "This doesn't seem like any cave I ever heard of."

Caves, Ben knew, formed within soluble rocks, carved out over centuries by water. This tunnel appeared to be a burrow. As his eyes traveled over the dirt walls, he remembered the huge bugs from the jungle interior, and he shuddered.

Thunder bowled through the island interior again. The outside air, redolent of ozone, salt water, and the soaked, fecund jungle floor, pushed into the tunnel as the wind rushed at them. When the cool raindrops splashed against their faces, they instinctively slid several yards deeper into the tunnel. The darkness did not recede as they moved toward its border. If anything it seemed to press closer, almost a living thing. The earthen walls felt like cold, dead hands on their backs.

Matt was seated closest to the gloom, his shoulder butting up against the darkness. Ben crouched over and moved around him, so that he was the first line of defense should anything rush out of the darkness at them. But as he put his foot down, icy fear gripped him—there was no ground under his foot.

Before he could catch his balance, Ben slid downward. Matt saw nothing in the blackness. Nothing except the faint ghost of his father, eyes wide, mouth locked in a silent scream, his face a witch mask. Matt reached for his father, but he was gone faster than his screaming voice could die against the earthen walls.

"Dad! Dad!"

Then silence. Dead silence.

**

Matt inched forward, careful not to drop over the unseen cliff. His heart pounded, his head thrumming so hard he thought he might faint. He couldn't see a thing. All about him, the air had taken on a horrible odor, like decaying animals. The blackness before him was palpable, like some gelatinous alien dimension that his father had vanished into. He thought that if he stuck his arm into the gloom, it would be enveloped in something wet and toxic.

A scream poised at his lips, yet Matt could not scream, for he was frozen where he stood, crippled by sensory overload. His father—vanished into the bowels of the earth. Himself, stranded with no idea where he was or if he would ever see another living soul.

He inched forward, his feet sliding through loose soil that felt sticky, almost like walking on fly paper.

"D-Dad?"

Something grabbed his ankle. He screamed.

"It's okay, Matt. It's me."

The relief that poured through Matt was so thorough that he nearly crumbled.

"I thought…thought you -"

"I slid down into the tunnel. It's on a sharp diagonal. Too sharp for me to crawl out of on my own. I'll need you to give me a hand."

Matt bent down toward his father's hand—the grip vise-tight around his ankle—toward where his father's voice seemed to rise out of the earth. Just as he was about to grip his father's wrist, he pulled his hand back. A dark thought crossed his mind—*what if that isn't my father. What if my father is dead and the voice I hear is the devil that pulled him down that hole.*

"C'mon, Matt. I can't hold on much longer."

Matt grasped his father's wrist with both hands and pulled. As his feet dug into the soft earth, he felt his father's body struggling to pull out of the tunnel.

"A little further, Matt. Almost…"

Matt dug in harder, leaning back, feeling the veins in his neck tighten like wound springs. Then Ben was out of the tunnel, panting on the earthen floor, as thunder rolled from the ocean into the gloom.

Lightning flashed—three rapid strokes that lit the tunnel interior like a strobe light. Matt, looking past his father, fell backward into the murky light at the tunnel entrance. Ben saw Matt's face turn chalk-white, his mouth hanging open as though he wanted to yell but had forgotten how to form words.

The three strobed flashes, snapshots of some amusement park haunted house ride come to life, left Matt without a firm grip on reality. He had seen…surely his eyes must have played tricks…no, he had seen a *man*—empty sockets for eyes, body dessicated as though something had drained the lifeblood out of him—cocooned to the tunnel wall beyond the drop off. A silken web stretched across his body, descending into the tunnel. The intricate pattern and the sheer size of the webbing were familiar to him. He had seen the same pattern enveloping the palms where the hawk had been wrapped like so much pigskin. He had seen the gaping hole in the dead man's chest cavity, long, hairless legs rising out of the orifice like the demon fingers of a ghoul crawling out of an open grave.

"Matt. What is it?"

Matt stared toward his father's voice, seeing only darkness, praying that the lightning would not penetrate the tunnel interior again.

"Matt. Talk to me. What happened?"

"Get away from there, Dad."

"What—"

"Get out of the tunnel!"

As Ben crawled toward the gray, a skittering sound came from the earthen ceiling. Something hissed behind him, like gas escaping. A spider, bigger than any spider Ben had ever believed could exist, shot down from the top of the tunnel on a nearly invisible strand of web. It was hairless like a black widow, as big as a softball, eight legs dancing maniacally as it descended.

Ben screamed in disgust and terror, trying to pull his arm away from the spider's path. The spider was too fast. Fangs like daggers penetrated flesh on the top of Ben's right hand. He whipped his arm, and the thing flew back into the darkness, hissing. Ben cried out as though acid were eating into his flesh. A fiery pain shot up his arm, and his muscles spasmed.

"Dad! What was that thing?"

Matt pulled his father by the arm into the driving rain, no longer caring about the thunderstorm. Ben crawled on all fours out of the tunnel, his right arm shaking like the legs of a newborn pony. He turned to face the tunnel, the rain thrumming down on his head. Something hissed from within the darkness, and he darted back from the tunnel opening.

Matt grabbed his father's right hand. Two deep incisions, already a sickly purple and pus-filled, marked where the spider had struck. Ben looked at his hand—which looked more like a clown's hand now than a human's—and averted his eyes.

"Jesus."

"Was that thing…is it poisonous?"

"How the hell should I know?" Ben breathed heavily as water ran in rivulets down his face. His eyes softened. "I'm sorry…sorry, Matt. Hell, I don't even know what kind of spider that was."

"How does your arm feel?"

"My arm?" Ben looked down his arm. A redness, almost like a fever rash, had spread from the base of his wrist to just shy of his elbow. "It…burns. Goddammit. It's like my skin is on fire."

Matt pulled his waterlogged t-shirt over his head; he wrapped it tightly about itself and tied it around his father's arm below the elbow.

"You think that will help?" Ben asked. Matt shook his head noncommittally. "In the tunnel…you saw something."

The little blood that had returned to Matt's face drained out again. He wanted to believe the lightning had fooled his eyes, that it had somehow evoked a waking nightmare out of him. His body shivering despite the oppressive humidity, he told his father what the lightning had revealed within the tunnel. Ben collapsed against the curved trunk of a palm.

"The boater," Matt whispered.

"Yeah," Ben said, eyes fixed on the blackened entrance.

Thunder roared once more, like a dinosaur resurrected. The storm sounded more distant now, the rain falling in smaller droplets. The eastern sky was black as night, while the western horizon was a volatile mixture of ragged, gray clouds and thin strands of sun vying for the ocean surface.

"The boat," Matt said. "Could we use the firewood we gathered as oars?"

As he watched the first God rays penetrate the clouds to turn the western waters golden, Ben clutched his right arm above the elbow. "One piece of wood against the ocean? Not likely. Not that I would know, bud. It's not like I ever tried to paddle across an ocean before."

"At least we'd be off the island," Matt said, looking warily back toward the tunnel.

Ben nodded, and the rain relented.

**

The spiders added a whole new element of danger to the jungle. Ben cringed at the thought of the island after dark. But it was a hell of a risk to take a boat without paddles into open waters. Once they were a hundred yards from shore, they would be at the whim of the ocean current. They could just as easily end up in the middle of the Atlantic, or fall off the edge of the earth, as find their way back to civilization.

"You know, there looked like there was a tiny bit of fuel left. Maybe enough to get us started and keep us going for five or ten minutes."

"How are you going to start the engine? We don't have the keys."

"I bet I know where the keys are," Ben said, staring intently into the tunnel.

Matt's eyes widened in realization. "No way, Dad. You can't go back in there."

Ben thought if he could fashion a torch and find a way to ignite it, he could get in and out of the tunnel quickly enough to avoid the spiders. As water poured off jungle leaves and cascaded onto the black, muddy earth, he knew there would be no easy way to get a fire started in this humidity.

Emerging from behind thinning clouds, the sun swept in flaxen tones across the rhythmic sea, turning the water to liquid gold. The orb, taking an accelerating westward track, was a deeper orange than it had been prior to the rains—almost bloody. Only a few hours of daylight remained.

"Okay. I'll have to find another way to start the engine."

Ben led Matt through the dripping jungle toward the shoreline. The sun felt strong above the canopy, but water spilled out of the leaves in buckets. Ben's eyes kept drifting through the tangle of green, searching for more telltale webbing. Once he had seen something glistening among a set of squat palms, its edges flashing like a mirage as a strand of sunlight penetrated the canopy. Then his forward movement took him past, and the jungle swallowed the view.

As the shoreline materialized through the thick jungle border, Ben leaned on Matt for support, his head swimming in a murky dizziness that was not the result of heat exhaustion. Matt looked at him with concern etched into his face.

"It's getting worse, isn't it?"

"I'll be fine. Just get me to that boat."

Taking care to walk through the shallows, they

stumbled along the shoreline, keeping several feet between them and the thick vegetation. As Matt and Ben continued southward, their shadows grew long, stretching across the shore toward the jungle's edge. Palms, which individually might have appeared idyllic in another setting, curved like hulking monsters in sentry formation along the wilderness periphery, the dying sun bathing them in bloody reds. Heavy, skittering noises rose out from the jungle interior. The sounds seemed to be moving closer.

The boat had taken on an additional inch of water but otherwise seemed exactly as they had left it. Ben climbed into the craft on trembling legs, feeling feverish. He sensed Matt's eyes on him, but there was no time for worry. He had to think. *If* he could figure out how to hot-wire the boat, *if* the engine started, and *if* there was enough fuel to get them a few miles into the sea…

So many *ifs*. He bent low and yanked the key switch cover off.

As he studied the wiring, he thought about the trip out of St. Kitts. They had left westward, the sun on their backs. After they became lost, Ben was sure the sun had generally been in his face or just off to his left as he attempted to reverse course. That meant he was probably somewhere south and west of his desired target. Trying to envision a map of the islands, he believed a straight westward track would lead them into the middle of nowhere. A northeastward track had the highest potential to get them back to St. Kitts or one of the nearby islands. A north-northeast track would run them close to Puerto Rico or the Dominican Republic if they were lucky. Straight south would run them into Venezuela, but that trip would take days, and they had no way to steer the boat once the motor died.

Steer the boat. Of course!

Ben looked behind him. A long paddle was attached to the interior side, so obvious that he was surprised the oar hadn't detached itself from the hull and smacked him on the ass. He bent his head back and laughed. Even if he couldn't get the boat to start, he had an oar. Seeing what his father had centered his eyes on, Matt snatched the oar from the side of the boat.

"This will work, right?"

"Hell, yes. It won't be easy paddling through ocean waves, but we'll make do."

Ben studied the variegated spaghetti strands of colored wires, his right arm still burning as though he had been injected with jet fuel. At least his head was beginning to clear. As he fumbled with the wires, Matt stared longingly at the oar and gave it a few practice strokes through the shallows. Multi-colored fish swam away from the oar, darting away from shore as though fired from a slingshot. While his father continued to sift through the wires, Matt spotted a red, plastic cup floating in the back corner of the boat. The top of one side of the cup had broken off, leaving behind a jagged bottom jaw of a Halloween pumpkin's grimace. The rest of the plastic was intact, so he busied himself bailing small amounts of water over the side of the boat.

As the sun accelerated toward the horizon, tall shadows crept across the shore. The shadows moved on the periphery of Ben's vision, and he might not have given them attention had his mind not alerted him that something was out of place. With the sun coming in from the west, the only shadows on the truncated beach should have been their own. His head lifted, and he gasped. Black spiders, hairless with orange and red markings that burned in the dying light, crept across the sand. Some were the size of tarantulas; others were colossal—the size of the largest bird eater spiders he had seen behind glass at the zoo. Within the mass of black crawled two unthinkable, spindly nightmares the lengths of house cats, creeping toward the boat like generals leading the march. Matt saw them, too, and he dropped the oar into the boat.

"Dad!"

Ben heard the fear in his son's voice at the same time that a hiss arose from the jungle's edge. He raised his head from the wires to see the horror spreading across the sand in a sea of crimson and black. There were dozens upon dozens, perhaps hundreds. His eyes moved across the advancing army, spotting eight-legged monstrosities whose fangs were visible from halfway across the beach.

"They can't reach us. They can't swim," Ben said, his words sounding more like a desperate hope than a statement of fact.

"Start the engine!"

"I can't yet...I don't know which—"

The words froze in Ben's mouth at the sight of a spider the length of a sewer rat rearing up on its hind legs and jumping several feet across the water. It thudded against the side of the boat as though someone had fired a softball at the hull. Ben grasped the rope knotted to the bow. He fumbled with the knot, seeing out of the corner of his eye the sand being overrun by throngs of spiders. Something heavier struck the hull.

Holding the oar like a weapon, Matt bent over the boat to witness a tangle of black legs rippling the water as a huge form was dragged under by the tide.

The spiders came from everywhere now: descending out of palms, scurrying beneath ferns, darting out of the black jungle like soldiers breaking out of their camouflage. Struggling to undo the knot, Ben stared in half-terror, half-amazement as dozens of spiders turned on each other, tearing one another apart as if to stake claim on the human targets in the boat.

From the outer hull came a vile scratching, like fingers clawing against the inside of a crypt. When Matt turned toward the sound, he saw two long, black, alien legs rising above the edge. The two legs extended over the hull, gripping the interior. Fangs, dripping with a milky substance, appeared over the edge. The spider, at least a foot in length, was about to drop into the boat when Matt swung the oar. The impact felt solid, as though the oar had struck a large animal. The spider was strong, too. Not falling over the side, the spider slid several inches across the top of the hull and turned toward Matt, ready to spring. The oar struck again. The blow swept the spider off the ledge and into the salty Atlantic, where its legs thrashed and its body spasmed as the tide pulled it out to sea.

Two more thuds slammed against the side of the boat. The hissing grew louder, as though live wires were writhing along the sand, spurting sparks into the failing daylight.

Ben worked the knot loose enough to slip a finger into its center. He started pulling the knot free when a grapefruit-sized spider with fiery orange striations leaped upward and latched itself to his left arm. Fangs pierced skin, and Ben felt the pain of a hundred wasps stinging as one. As he tried to push it off with his hand, he saw it rear back, preparing to launch itself at his face. In a moment frozen in time, he saw his own witch mask reflected in its eight eyes.

Matt was by Ben's side immediately, swatting the spider off his father's arm with the oar. Ben yanked the end of the rope through the knot, freeing the boat. As the rope fell away, Ben noticed an elongated abomination—almost squid-like—climbing across the rope, its legs wrapped around the synthetic fibers. The thing hit the wet sand with a splatter, and it scurried angrily to its belly.

Scratching sounds came from both sides of the boat's exterior like a family of rats rustling through hollow walls. Long, black legs—dozens upon dozens—crept over the sides. Matt cocked back the oar just as the squid-like spider launched itself over the water's edge onto the boy's back. Fangs buried themselves into Matt's shoulders—the thing biting, and biting, and biting again—rapidly turning his skin into something that looked like hamburger meat. Ben snatched the oar out of his son's hands, forcibly prying the spider off his son's shoulders. Seeing bits of his son's flesh in the spider's fangs caused Ben to gag.

As though sensing triumph, the black army swarmed over the sides of the boat. The hissing that arose from the beach almost sounded desperate, as though the gathering throng feared there would be nothing left of the man and boy when the remaining spiders reached the boat.

For every spider Ben swatted with the oar, several more spilled into the boat. His arms shaking and his body trembling from the venom racing through his blood, Ben was barely able to stay on his feet. Driven by survival instinct, he swung the oar at anything that moved. The boat interior was filled with the sickening crunch of the oar against their bodies, like crab shells cracking. The force of the blows sent spiders rocketing against the fiberglass sides, some breaking open on impact, guts and milkweed-like secretions oozing out of their skin. Others landed on the backs, legs flailing madly as they suffered their death throes.

But there were so many.

Dizzy and nauseous from the spider's attack, Matt stumbled weaponless across the boat as more spiders sprung toward him. One landed on his left arm, and before he could knock it off, a monstrous, ink-black spider attached itself to his right arm, digging switchblade-fangs into his flesh. The abomination wrapped its legs around the center of his arm, bear hugging him so Matt could not bend his elbow. The spider skittered upward, not releasing its python grip, inching toward Matt's neck.

Ben felt the boat shake as something crashed to the floor. He half-expected to see a spider the size of a wolf, but what he saw when he turned was even more terrifying. Matt was face down on the floor, gurgling in the shallow water, as a mass of spiders swarmed over his body. The boy's legs twitched.

Head swimming, Ben somehow maintained balance as he swung the oar against the spiders crawling across Matt's body. The spiders scattered across the boat with each swipe, only to turn and immediately resume the attack. Ben thought to lay himself atop Matt as a human shield; but he knew that if he did so, they would both be overwhelmed. Ben saw a nightmare image of Matt and him cocooned on the boat floor, eyes lifeless, as spindly legs skittered across their bodies, fangs drawing blood until their bodies were dessicated, skeletal shells.

His arms seemed to swing the oar on their own. For a moment, he felt disembodied, as though he were watching the desperate battle from afar. The bottom of the boat was covered with broken spider bodies, abdomens split open, pouring forth pus.

He was vaguely aware that the boat had drifted a few feet off shore, advancing and retreating to and fro with the tide. He thought—or rather, he prayed—that the boat was too far offshore for the swarm of spiders on the beach to reach them. He hadn't heard them hitting the sides of the boat or skittering along the outer hull in the last minute. If he saw more of their legs appearing over the sides, he might go mad.

When a spider darted out of the stern toward his son's neck, Ben belted the hissing monster with the oar. It ripped through the air, clipping the edge of the outer wall as it flew into the Atlantic.

He felt eyes on his back, as though the cold breath of the undead had touched his skin. A loud hiss spun Ben around so that he was staring at the mammoth spider that had attacked Matt. Its front legs raised into the air, and Ben saw it lean back, ready to spring. Another spider came at Ben from the side, and he swatted it away, never taking his eyes off the black Goliath in front of him. He raised the oar, daring the beast to come for him.

The spider leaped at him, its weight rocking the boat. In a moment of frozen time, he saw its razor fangs, dripping with venom, his pallid reflection mirrored as eight distinct ghosts in the spider's eyes, its front legs hooked over, ready to latch itself onto him. He swung the oar in blind desperation. He made solid contact, but it felt as though the oar had struck a tree trunk. Fear screamed through his body, as he heard the oar snap.

The boat, the ocean, and then the sky wheeled past his eyes in a dizzying view from an amusement park ride. As he was driven backward, his head struck the side of the boat. The spider scrambled atop him, smothering his chest and neck in a swarm of legs. He saw his reflection in the eyes again—the reflection of a dead man. The spider lunged at his neck. He bucked upward, and the fangs missed their mark but tore through the underside of his chin like dual knives plunging into a soft underbelly.

He heard himself scream as the spider reared back. He felt its the venom burning under his skin, spreading into his face and down his neck as if his flesh was afire. His arms spasming, he thought in frigid terror that the venom would paralyze him. No longer able to fight back, he knew he was going to die.

As though in slow motion, he saw the beast's front legs raise into the air, spider eyes centering on his. Blood, his blood, dripped off the spider's fangs like the crimson maw of a ravenous vampire.

The spider sprung at his face—a black, alien nightmare. He closed his eyes.

It crashed down on his upper chest, well short of its intended target. Teetering on the edge of consciousness, he was vaguely aware of the spider twitching, grotesquely spasming atop him. His eyes shut, seeing the world awash in reds and pinks through closed eyelids. The spider seemed to be pressing down on his chest with greater force, though strangely the infernal hissing had ceased, and the razor fangs were not tearing the flesh off of his bones. *I must already be dead*, he thought.

His eyes squinted open, and just before he drifted into unconsciousness, he saw the glint of the descending sun in the spider's lifeless eyes, the broken shaft of the oar impaled in its abdomen, Matt standing over the spider, insanity in the boy's eyes...

**

He awoke to a patchwork quilt of a million stars.

The keening of the ocean breeze rippled the water's surface, which sparkled as a mirror image of the midnight sky. He tried to lift his head, but it felt as though it was weighted down by sandbags.

"Dad?"

Ben turned his head toward the voice. Matt knelt beside him.

"Where are we?"

"Heading northeast according to the compass." Matt held the broken oar, pointing at the paddle end. "It still works."

"You did good, son. Real good."

The broken oar.

Ben twitched and brushed his hands down his body at invisible attackers.

"Spiders..."

"No," Matt said, placing his hands on his father's chest to keep him still. "They're dead. They're all dead. Rest a little longer. We'll find our way home tomorrow."

Home.

Ben lay his head back against the wet floor of the boat. The craft rocked to a soothing ocean lullaby. The moon, three-quarters full, bathed the endless sea in azure tones from horizon to horizon. He closed his eyes.

**

Ben didn't recall awakening to the thin strip of

predawn gray light, bubbling out of the eastern waters. Matt, knees pulled up to his chest and head resting against the hull, saw his father rise zombie-like, shuffling, stumbling, and careening off the sides of the boat until he reached the colored spaghetti wires. The venom no longer seemed to be advancing, and though Ben appeared incognizant, he had sufficient strength to drag himself to the wheel.

Matt watched with wonder as his father, eyes closed as though he were sleepwalking, played his hands through the myriad strands of wire like a blind, idiot savant. Matt leaned his head back against the boat and closed his eyes. He was not the least bit surprised by the sound of the motor roaring to life. He laughed, thinking at that moment that his father was the same superhero he had considered him to be as a child, capable of anything. When Matt's eyes squinted open, he saw his father—eyes still shut as they drifted between the wheel, the compass, and the water as though he were receiving signals from radio waves—queerly navigating the boat to the northeast.

Matt let the broken oar fall out of his hands. He knew he would not be needing it anymore. As reassuring comfort spread through him, he drifted into sleep.

**

When Ben awakened to distant shouting, the sun was at its midmorning position over the ocean, the warm, orange coloration already giving way to a fiery white. He glanced over at Matt, the boy's head resting on his shoulders. The waves were louder and hollow sounding, as if his ear was pressed to a seashell. The shouting grew closer, louder. Ben wasn't sure what the voices were yelling, but he was pretty sure they were speaking Spanish.

He had just enough strength to cock his head over the side of the boat.

Land. Beautiful land.

A motorboat full of three dark-skinned men raced toward them, their boat bouncing over waves like a wheelie-popping motorcycle. He drifted unconscious momentarily and then was reawakened by a sun-parched face breathing over him.

"Where are we?" Ben asked in a hoarse whisper.

"Que?"

"St. Croix," said an unseen man who apparently understood English.

"My wife. St. Kitts," Ben muttered.

"No problem. We get you home. First to shore and hospital."

The English speaking man climbed into the boat and stayed with Ben and Matt while the other motorboat dragged their craft to shore. Ben heard him talking to Matt about something—baseball, he thought, and if the Yankees were going to make the playoffs—but it was all mired in the fog of semi-sleep. He felt sea spray on his face and their boat riding continuously up and over waves, like the never ending humps of a wooden roller coaster track.

Then he was being helped to his feet, off the boat and onto a beach, the sunlight like a nuclear blast against his sensitive eyes.

A siren wailed in the distance—a little different sound than the ambulances made back home, Ben thought. He heard concerned murmurs as people massed around them, many of the voices from fellow vacationing Americans.

Ben glanced back at the motorboat one last time as his feet sank into wet sand. Stumbling forward onto hard shells, he shivered. He saw the web glistening beneath the wheel, extending along the bow. It sparkled in the strengthening sun, rippling with the sea breeze like a bed sheet hung to dry by clothespins. He spied something darker hanging back behind the web, hunkered down like a lion on the Savannah, biding its time. Ben pointed toward the web as his legs buckled beneath him. He was clutched

32

by another set of arms and whisked toward the ambulance.

**

    Ben and Matt received intravenous fluids throughout the afternoon at a tiny hospital where no one but a few doctors spoke English.

    Relieved, Marie arrived shortly after supper, firing admonitions that if they were ever to take a boat into unfamiliar waters again, they would have to answer to her. The doctor overseeing Ben and Matt, a grandfatherly man who spoke Spanish, Creole, and English, gave the clearance for them to be released with Marie that evening.

    The doctor listened to their stories of the attacking spiders, examining the myriad puncture wounds covering their bodies. Perhaps the two Americans had stumbled into a den of tarantulas. Certainly their memories were exaggerated by the stress of being lost at sea and weathering the tropical heat without adequate protection. The nurse, a native islander who spoke no English, rubbed a salve over their punctured flesh, her eyes barely containing her building terror as she subconsciously estimated what size of spider could have produced the abnormally large wound spacings.

**

    At 8:30, as a soothing balm of mystical twilight dripped over the islands, the disabled motorboat—tied to a pier near the edge of the tourist beach—bobbed and danced to the tempo of the black and silver sea. Two young brothers played in the sand, the slightly older boy laying a bucket face down on the edge of a crude sandcastle kingdom. Removing the bucket, he smiled contentedly at the wet, molded turret which completed the masterpiece.

    As the boys' mother yelled at them for the last time to

pack their gear, the younger brother crafted tiny holes for windows with his fingers, wondering what the fuss was about. The mother watched the shadows of the pier stretch like gnarled fingers across the sand toward her children, eyes fixed warily on the boat which slid on the tide between sand and water. Something unsettled her about the boat, which appeared oddly dangerous in the dying light.

Now the shadows raced across water and sand, like ink pouring out of the heavens. She realized with sudden panic that she could no longer see her children, who were swallowed whole by the encroaching darkness. She called again, and as the frantic edge in her voice cut through the gloom, something spilled over the side of the boat onto the wet sand. A black mass of writhing legs reached into the night air; it flipped itself over to its stomach and crept toward the kingdom of sand. The bloated spider was huge, very hungry, and very pregnant. It lunged toward the shapes surrounding the castle, fangs dripping with venom, just as the woman's hands reached forward to drag her protesting children away from the water.

As she hurried the children off the beach toward the ocher lights of their resort, she heard a hissing sound, like the sand had opened up to a pit of snakes. Something skittered across the beach behind them, moving toward the deeper shadows of lush flora between the beach and the resort. The woman dragged the boys along faster, not stopping when the younger brother lost his flip-flops or when the older brother stumbled over the smooth planks of the palm-lined boardwalk.

She ran with held breath, convinced that the devil himself had emerged from the ocean waters, not stopping to breathe until she and the boys were inside the resort, doors closed to the night. As her children bleated over stubbed toes and lost shoes, she looked into the mass of ferns and palm fronds. There was something creeping through the shadows. She rushed the boys toward the elevator doors, desperate to put more walls between her and the night.

Treman Mills

The silver wood screws holding the board in place looked new compared to the rusty, flaking pieces which clasped the neighboring panels.

"So what if they're new?" Rachel asked Charlie.

Wishing Charlie would give up on his fixation, she stood hands-on-hips, one eye watching the setting sun, blonde hair dancing in the breeze. She rubbed the goosebumps off her arms, appreciating how quickly the day's heat disappeared in upstate New York during late September.

"I'll tell you why," Charlie said. "It means this panel was replaced recently. Kinda fishy for a boarded up building. Don't you enjoy a good mystery?"

The brownstone high-rise stretched up and up into the fading light, standing a full story above its tallest neighbors. Weathered boards concealed old, shattered windows like eye patches. A crisscross of planks covered the doorway, where a wind-torn KEEP OUT sign was stapled above the knob.

"I really don't care, Charlie. Let's just go."

As a faded strip of newspaper drifted like a ghost across the vacant street, the rumble of motors and a car horn sounded in the distance, making Rachel wish she were at the center of town near people, stores, lights, and safety. Anywhere but the north side of Treman Mills, New York, with its abandoned buildings and shadowed alleyways. Fires twenty years ago had crippled the once-thriving section of town. The north side tried to rebuild a decade ago, but the big box retailers had moved into the center of town and stolen what little commerce remained. Now it was a ghost town, a blight, a location even the drug traffickers and gangs did their best to avoid.

The sun vanished behind twin tower apartments on

the far side of downtown. Shadows crept down from the building tops.

"I knew we shouldn't have come this way," Rachel said, eyeing a vintage Chevy Impala parked up the road, its windshield littered with yellow tickets and the back bumper askew.

Spray-painted gang symbols and vulgar words marred the exterior. *Why haven't the police towed it away?* Rachel wondered. *Doesn't anyone care?*

They were both seniors at Treman Mills Central School, she the smartest girl in Chemistry Club, he the strongest boy on the football team. Their conformity to stereotypes might have kept them apart perpetually had they not grown up three houses away from one another. For as long as Rachel could remember, she and Charlie had walked home from school together. Or more to the point, he'd walked her home, because he was a strong boy, and Daddy wanted the strongest boy to watch over his little girl, and now he was a football star, and Daddy loved football most of all, so…

And for just as long as she'd know Charlie, she'd known him to be pig-headed and stubborn once he set his mind to something.

"You're supposed to be home before seven," Charlie said, trying to squeeze his fingers between board and building.

His light brown hair was laden with sweat, matted to his forehead. While he chewed a hunk of gum that appeared to be the size of a tennis ball, he threw his blue football jacket over his shoulder. A trustworthy color, blue was; Rachel once read that a blue suit could influence someone to trust the smiling face on the television. Blue swayed juries, gave people a sense of peace and serenity when all hell was breaking loose.

Do I trust you, Charlie?

"Seven, or my parents will freak."

37

"This is the only route to get from school to home and still make it on time."

"I'll be late anyways if you keep screwing around—"

Bang!

Charlie struck the board, which rattled like stage thunder.

He has a violent streak, too, she thought, remembering the time he'd beaten Nate Kerns within an inch of his life because he'd caught Nate flirting with his girlfriend.

Her next protest was on her lips when Charlie pulled a multi tool from his backpack and began wrenching the screws counterclockwise.

"Are you crazy? You can't break into an abandoned building. It's against the law."

"Gosh, you're right." He pantomimed panic, glancing wide-eyed up and down the street, and said, "Oh, I forgot. Nobody cares about the north side." He spat on the sidewalk and yelled at the top of his lungs. "You hear me Treman Mills? Nobody fucking cares!"

She looked down her nose at him. "Are you through?"

"If I set the building on fire, it's a 50-50 bet that the fire department will show up at all."

"Which you wouldn't do." After a pregnant pause, she asked, "Would you?"

He stood in silence, as though considering his words. "Arson is an impersonal crime."

Working fervently on the sticky screw, he pulled the gum from his mouth and stuck it to the side of the building. To her revulsion, he jammed his thumb into the gum and left his print, Charlie's Neanderthal way of marking territory.

"Do you have to be so gross?"

In school, Charlie's gum thumb print could be found on the backs of chairs, on lockers, under desks, and for the truly unfortunate and bullied, tangled in locks of hair. He glared at her and cranked harder on the multi tool.

With a fingernails-on-chalkboard squeal, the top left screw popped out.

A pall fell over Rachel, as though Charlie were prying open a tomb.

"Why are you trying to break in? I hope it isn't to do something stupid. Vandalism will get you kicked off the football team, maybe even suspended from school."

Smiling over his shoulder, he said, "Vandalism? That's little league stuff. You know me better than that."

Do I?

As he dropped his arm in exhaustion and wiped sweat from his brow, he sighed. "Don't you know what this building used to be?"

"Not really."

"Foreman Games and Sports Cards. My old man says Foreman's business was so successful that he purchased the floor above the store for storage, so the first two floors are his."

"*Were* his. Didn't the building burn to the ground twenty years ago?"

"Not this one. A lot of these other buildings did," Charlie said, gesturing down the darkened corridor of buildings. "But not Foreman's. Old Foreman had a heart attack and keeled over while business was still booming. Who knows what he left behind? I might find a Mickey Mantle or Ted Williams card."

"Who?"

Charlie threw up his hands in exasperation. "Who? You're worse than my sister."

"I'm kidding. I know who Mickey Mantle and Ted Williams are."

Eyeing her skeptically, he went back to work on the upper right screw, which hung halfway out of the board.

"Anyhow, if I find anything valuable, I can sell it online

and get a down payment on a car."

"You haven't gotten your license yet."

He shrugged. "Doesn't matter. I want the money. And besides, I bet you want to know why these screws are new, and who replaced this board. Someone has been coming in and out of this building."

Sweat pouring down her back, Rachel worried about drug addicts and dealers hiding inside.

Bleeding around the corners of distant buildings, the final embers of the sun kissed the horizon. Two men shouted from a few blocks off, and the black shadow of a vulture winged through the sky. Darkness crept toward the abandoned buildings.

"If you don't stop, I'm walking home without you."

Charlie ignored her, chewing his lower lip as he wrestled with the multi tool. Three screws removed, he was hard at work on the final screw when Rachel turned her back and began to walk away.

"Wait." He grabbed hold of the back of her shirt. "You can't go."

Arms folded, she spun to face him.

"Take your hands off of me."

Wringing his hands, he looked nervously up and down the street. "Stop shouting. You'll attract unwanted attention."

"I'm not kidding around. You know how dangerous this town is after dark."

"Don't believe everything you read in the newspapers. Reporters exaggerate everything."

"Five people missing in less than a year."

She stared daggers at him, and he flinched. Charlie played the tough guy around his friends, but a few harsh words from Rachel were always enough to send Charlie backpedaling.

"You know how many people go missing in New York City every month?" he asked.

"No. Do you?"

"A lot," he said, stammering as though he'd wished he hadn't given her the chance to corner him on facts and statistics.

"Charlie Tanner, there are less than twenty-thousand people in Treman Mills. Five missing is a really big deal."

"The cops don't seem too concerned."

"The cops have their hands in the donut box and their heads up their asses ."

The corner of Charlie's mouth curled into a smile, and he started to giggle. Infectious laughter spread, and soon Charlie was red-faced and doubled over, clutching his ribs.

"It really wasn't that funny," she said.

"Hands in the donut box and heads up their asses?" He could barely speak, he laughed so hard.

Then the laughter suddenly stopped, and he slammed his shoulder into the panel.

"Fucking pigs."

Shaken by the sudden personality swing, she edged away from him. Charlie went back to unscrewing the panel, as though nothing had happened, his backpack strewn on the sidewalk under his feet.

"Seriously," she said, a nervous waver in her voice. "It would be horrible enough if five people were found murdered. But to completely disappear…how does one hide five bodies?"

"You've got fifteen miles of forest and wetlands north of town. Plenty of places to hide a body. But you're assuming people were murdered. Maybe they just got sick of this place and left. It's not against the law to leave Treman Mills. Two of the missing were community college students, you know? Maybe they decided to take Daddy's tuition money and hitchhike across Europe for a year."

Before she replied, the last screw whirred out of the board. With a grunt, Charlie hoisted the panel and shoved it aside.

A darkness blacker than midnight rolled out of the opening; Rachel backed away. Stale air laced with something redolent of chemicals and poison wafted out. It was as though the big building exhaled.

Death. She could think of no better word for what infested the building's dark corridors.

Her instinctual voice urged her to run. Boarded up windows glared down on her, yet the opening looked less like an eye than it did a mouth. The window glass was broken out.

Probably lying in a heap under the sill. When I step on the glass, it will sound like brittle bones crumbling.

The squeal of tires and thump of a car stereo woofer brought their heads around.

"Sounds like bad company," he said, looking uneasily down the avenue.

Funny that a town so small could have so many big city dangers, Rachel thought.

The pounding bass grew closer. Maybe it wasn't funny at all.

"That's Thorn's car," she whispered.

Steven Rollo, known to everyone as Thorn—the police alleged he was one of the county's largest drug dealers—led a violent gang called the Black Thorns. Only three years older than Rachel, Thorn had gotten himself expelled in the tenth grade for pulling a knife on Mr. Bischoff, the school biology teacher. Yet Thorn had never struck Rachel as the violent type. In fact he'd once directed her to class when she was a lost sixth grader, hopelessly looking for her math room.

What went wrong with Thorn? What turned him violent?

One thing was for sure—she would be in danger if the Black Thorns saw her in this section of town with no police within five city blocks.

"I ain't afraid of Thorn," Charlie said, feigning indifference. She noticed his body had shifted so he could make a mad dash for the corner if Thorn's red El Camino came rolling around the corner. "Still think your teddy bear is harmless?"

She glared at him. "When have I ever called him a teddy bear? I just don't believe he's nearly as dangerous as the police say he is."

"Yeah? Well, the Black Thorns nearly beat that guy to death last summer just because he wouldn't sell them booze. Think the newspapers lied about it?"

"They never proved it was the Black Thorns. Was there an arrest?"

"It's like you said. The cops have their heads up their asses. They never catch the bad guy. By the way, what was it Thorn used to call you before he became America's most wanted? Water bug?" He nearly spat the nickname.

"Yeah," she whispered.

"Why the hell would he call you water bug?"

Rachel shrugged, though she recalled darting among students racing between classes, so much smaller than the upperclassmen.

She checked her watch, which read twenty minutes until seven, twenty minutes until her parents would ground her if she didn't beat curfew.

The metronomic bass thump faded into downtown. Rachel exhaled.

As the darkness and stench rolled out of the open window, her skin crawled with goosebumps.

"Game's over. The board is off, and you've looked inside. Let's go home."

"I just want to take a quick look around. You don't have to come if you don't want to."

"I *don't* want to."

"No problem. I can go by myself. I'll be back before

you can count to thirty. Or maybe a hundred."

"You're not leaving me alone on the street after sunset. Forget it."

"Then you're coming with me."

She shook her head and stared deep into that impenetrable darkness. Another scent drifted through the window—a dead smell. When she was twelve, she'd found a dead baby mouse inside an empty Coke bottle behind her shed, baked by the July sun. That was the scent she smelled now hidden behind the chemicals.

Rachel opened her mouth to tell him off when the El Camino screeched around the corner, music thundering.

"It's them," Charlie said, edging toward the window. Before she could turn and run, he leaped over the sill into the abandoned building and grabbed her waist.

"Charlie, no."

"They'll kill you if they see you. Hang on," he said, hoisting her up and pulling her inside.

She landed on a heap of debris. Shattered glass crunched under her feet as he yanked her away from the window and out of sight. They stood shoulder-to-shoulder, backs against spider-webbed walls, listening as the car rolled closer. Something fell into her hair—dust, insulation, rat feces, she couldn't be sure—and she banged her foot against an old broken-out television.

As Charlie spared a quick glance around the window's edge, she asked, "Who's out there?"

His lips curled into an ironic smile. "You damn well know who's out there. Your teddy bear and his thugs. And they're slowing down."

The woofer's bass rattled the walls and seeped into her bones. The vehicle was right outside the window.

Charlie looked around the edge again and quickly pulled back. "Shit!"

"Did they see you?"

"I think so." The wall of sound seemed to be on top of them. Sweat poured off Charlie's brow and beaded on his upper lip. "Oh shit, oh shit. What the hell am I gonna do?" She jumped when he pounded his fist against the wall. "Dammit. They're ruining—"

He closed his mouth as the music cut off with the engine. A car door opened and slammed shut. Boots scraped against macadam, approaching the open window. A long, black shadow interrupted the rectangle of fading light cast across the dingy floor.

Charlie grabbed her by the hand, and she ran willingly with him into the vast nothingness. She couldn't see her hand in front of her face, had no idea where the walls were or if something sharp and dangerous lay before her. As she stumbled along behind him, she feared she would run belly-first into a broken, jagged plank or drop through a hole in the floor. She looked behind her one last time to see the shadow growing. Before they turned the corner into a hallway, a hand marred by bruised knuckles and tattooed fingers grabbed hold of the sill.

Rachel's breaths fired rapid in her chest. The dead, dusty air she sucked in made her want to gag.

What am I doing here?

She should be home, curled on the couch with homework and snacking on dinner leftovers. If she died here, would anyone find her?

Charlie led her along a corridor, his hand feeling along the wall until he grasped hold of a doorknob. She could see nothing, but the echo of her footsteps told her they'd entered a stairwell.

"Slow down...I can't see. Where are you taking us?"

"Up a few floors." His breath was hot on her neck and smelled of onions and hamburger meat as he whispered into her ear. "We gotta hide. Just step quietly. I don't want them to know which way we went."

Would Thorn's gang kill them just for being on the

wrong side of town? She didn't think so, but Charlie started climbing, and she needed to keep up. Vertigo fell over her as she ascended, unable to see the stairs, every invisible step throwing off her equilibrium. Holding a rotted, wooden rail, she felt her hand scrape through a decade of accumulated dust. A myriad of splinters penetrated her skin. When she unknowingly reached the next landing, her legs kept trying to climb, and she fell into Charlie's back.

"Careful," he said.

A dull thud sounded below. Someone was on the first floor.

Halfway up the next set of stairs, her foot buckled on a shard of metal debris that made a grating noise, and her ankle twisted. She bit back a scream and grasped hold of the back of his shirt, thinking if she lost him in the dark she'd go mad.

Just hold on. He knows where he's going.

Please, God. Let him know where he's going.

They'd climbed two or three flights of stairs without a shred of light when Charlie stopped and opened another door.

"This way," he said.

Below, heavy-booted footsteps moved across the ground floor.

As hard as Rachel strained her eyes, she couldn't see anything but blackness. The sturdy floor under her feet was the only evidence that she wasn't about to walk off the edge of the world. Somehow Charlie managed to see, for he pulled her through the door and down a long hallway. She noticed how silently he moved, surprising for such a large boy.

If the air on the first floor was stagnant, the airflow here was crypt-like, the death scent stronger. She remembered walking blindly through a Halloween haunted house last year and how unsettling it was to see nothing but darkness. She'd walked into walls, bumped her knee on unexpected obstacles. And once a hand had reached out of the shadows and grabbed her bare ankle. She'd screamed then. If an unknown hand grabbed her now, her heart would burst. Unlike the haunted house, there was no one to turn on the lights and save her if she couldn't find her way out.

This can't be happening.

She thought she heard a voice from below.

"How can you see?"

"Don't worry. I'll get you to someplace where nobody will find—"

The stairwell door opened and echoed shut.

"Come on," he said, moving faster down the endless hallway.

Footsteps crept up through the stairwell.

Her heart raced faster. She saw white spots before her eyes, felt faint.

The footsteps were closer. As the door creaked open behind her, he suddenly pulled her into a room.

He edged the door shut, careful not to make a sound, and threw a rusty bolt into the latch.

In this room she could finally see; the panel had rotted and fallen away from the window and lay shattered in the parking lot below. The sun was down and the moon up, the sky a dusky bruised color through a grimy window dotted by bird excrement. At least the scent of decay, overwhelming at this end of the hallway, was not as strong—breaks in the window, where moths buzzed in and out, allowed her to breathe the night air.

She checked her watch. It was twelve minutes after seven. By now her father would have decided upon her grounding, and her mother would be arguing for leniency.

Mom. Dad. I'm so close to you, only three blocks away. Please come. Please help.

Charlie stood, chest heaving with his back pressed to the door. Biting down on her lower lip until she drew blood,

Rachel figured it was better to focus on pain than allow herself to cry. Someone was down the hallway, jiggling and testing door knobs. Light sweeping the hallway bled through cracks in the weathered door.

He has a flashlight.

If Thorn knew they were hiding on this floor, they were trapped. If she broke the window, it was a three story fall to a parking lot riddled with broken bottles. Craning her head between jagged pieces of glass, she inhaled the fresh air and examined the building's exterior. No panels had fallen off of the lowest two floors and given her an additional escape route, though adjacent rooms on the third floor were missing panels, too. An old wire fence leaned directly beneath the window, rusty barbed wire strung along its top.

Charlie's eyes were squeezed shut; his lips uttered a silent prayer.

Footsteps approached. Old boards groaned under heavy weight.

She accepted it was Thorn out in the hallway, for she'd seen the El Camino and recognized the gang symbols on the tattooed hand.

But he wouldn't kill me. I know he wouldn't. He knew me once, and he'll remember me. He's not a murderer.

Sweat poured off Charlie's forehead and cut streaks into his dusty face. He breathed so heavily that Rachel was sure he'd give them away if not have a heart attack. Outside the door the footsteps sounded closer, heavier. Rachel held her breath and waited for the doorknob to turn. If Thorn found the door locked, he'd have the rest of the Black Thorns surround the room and block their escape out the window. Or maybe he'd shoot into the door and blast holes through Charlie.

When it seemed they'd been found, the footsteps suddenly stopped and reversed down the hallway. Charlie slumped down to his knees and ran a hand through sweaty hair. Moments later the stairwell door opened and shut.

Footfalls descended the stairs.

As Rachel started to speak, Charlie put his forefinger to his lips and cut her off.

"Shh. He hasn't left the building yet."

They sat in silence as the minutes ticked by. Dusk at the window grew darker. Rachel's watch read 7:30—both her mother and father would be angry with her now. In another hour, her father would phone the police to report her missing, and she could only pray the police would take the matter seriously. She began to regret her quip about Tremen Mills cops and donuts.

I'll be home by then. Just as soon as we're sure the Black Thorns are out of the building, I can finally get out of this place.

She caught Charlie staring at her in the blue light of the moon. She didn't like his beady eyes, the way he glared at her like she was less than human.

"It's not my fault," she whispered back at him. "I want to get out of here just as much as you do."

Her voice broke his trance, and he moved his gaze to the window.

She started to rise out of her crouch, and he said, "Sit."

The edge to his voice bothered her. Not entirely trusting his state of mind, she did as she was told. More minutes passed without evidence that Thorn was still in the building. Sometimes a floorboard groaned. Other times grit trickled down from above, as though the ceiling was about to fall down on them. She watched the old building slowly fall to pieces.

All the more reason to get out of here before the floor collapses or something terrible happens.

The sky was black and the stars sharp, scattered like broken glass.

Charlie finally stood.

49

"Stay here. I'll make sure the coast is clear."

She challenged him with her glare, but he shrugged her off. Her heart pounded as he told her he'd be right back and slipped out the door.

The icy solitude bothered her immediately. While she could still hear him, she listened to the heavy steps of his sneakers moving down the long hallway, leaving her to face the dark alone. She wanted to throw the door open and rush after him. What if the Black Thorns were waiting in the stairwell?

She slipped the bolt into the latch.

Another vulture flew past the window. Distant traffic sounds seemed to come from the other side of the world. It was impossible for her not to think about her parents and how close home was. Looking out over the wasteland of neglected buildings and rundown neighborhoods, she could see the lights of Elm Street. One of those flares in the night was her porch light, though it was impossible to tell which one it was from this distance.

As a heavier silence fell over the building, she checked her watch and realized Charlie had been gone for almost twenty minutes; it was nearly eight o'clock. The idea of breaking the window and climbing down the building didn't sound so bad now. If she could gain a foothold on the sill and—

A loud thud sounded from one of the lower floors. Rachel jumped. The sound could've been anything, she told herself. Maybe it was falling debris or the groan of the old building settling.

Or Charlie's body hitting the floor after someone stuck a knife in his back.

The four walls seemed to close in on her. Below, the pounding came again.

She rushed to the window and looked down at the sheer drop into the pavement.

No chance. I'll be killed.

Charlie might be injured. Someone else might be inside the building. Reaching down, she sifted through pieces of shattered glass until she found a long, jagged piece. Cutting a cloth strip from the bottom of her shirt, she wrapped it around the lower part of the glass.

A loud, continuous pounding brought her head around.

Where? The first floor?

The stifled acoustics made noises seem to come from all parts of the building at once.

Creeping to the door, Rachel placed her ear against the panel. It was quiet now. Was someone on the other side of the door waiting?

Her palms sweating, she slid back the bolt, threw the door open, and thrust the shard into the hallway.

Nobody.

She closed the door behind her.

If someone is stalking us, better to make them believe I'm still hidden inside.

She held the makeshift weapon before her and moved down the hallway, invisible, wrapped in the withering specter of blackness. The return trip down the corridor was no more visible than the first, and she was forced to feel her way along moldy, rotting walls. The decay smell was overwhelming; she breathed through her mouth to lessen her nausea. When she touched another doorknob, she tested the door and found it unlocked. The door jammed in its frame, warped by years of humidity and neglect. Putting her shoulder into the door, she forced it open. Rotten wood broke off in chunks from the top and rained into her hair. Repulsed, she backed away as moonlight trickled into the hallway. Something skittered across her foot, and she stifled a squeal. A cockroach the size of a small rat raced up the wall.

The moonlight bought her another ten yards of murky visibility. Covering her mouth from the toxic dust motes floating around her, she crept down the hall. So dark was the passageway that she banged her nose against the wall at the end of the hall, completely missing the stairwell. She froze, praying she hadn't been heard.

What little moonlight seeped down the hallway disappeared the moment she pulled open the stairwell door. She tried to swallow but found her mouth dry. Carefully she took one step down, then another. The door clicked shut behind her, and now the darkness was absolute. Chunks of wooden handrail broke off and disintegrated in her hand as she descended.

Turning at the landing, she plunged deeper into the dark. Her steps echoed dully. Dead sounds, like blood dripping off a cadaver. Cobwebs—she hoped they were cobwebs and not spiderwebs—caught in her hair and trailed down her back.

When she reached the stairwell bottom, she felt her way to the door and placed her ear against the rust-pocked exterior.

No sounds. No pounding.

Nothing.

The door betrayed her, groaning as she pulled it open.

She remembered this hallway, black as pitch. Though it petrified her to walk into the darkness, into the unknown, moonlight through the removed panel would allow her to see. She just needed to take the first step.

Walking with arms outstretched at her sides, she felt along the narrow passageway's walls. The death stench lessened, though she smelled it from above, as though the smell was part of the walls. She banged her knee against a metal cabinet. Something fell off the cabinet and clanged noisily.

Holding her breath, she ducked down and listened.

Still nothing.

The collision was proof she'd traversed the hallway.

Why can't I see?

Crawling to her feet, Rachel edged through the dark, hands extended in front of her, feeling for hidden dangers. She worried again about holes in the floor, but there was nothing to be done for it now. All the while she kept looking off toward where she believed the removed panel to be. No light. No sounds. Just her pulse thrumming in her ears and the dusty air crusting her lungs.

Everything seemed disturbing.

Something sharp and rusty tore her shirt. She walked face-first into a spiderweb, and something crawled down her back. All around her, skittering noises clawed inside the walls.

As she found her way along the street-side wall, the darkness interrupted by thin strips of street lighting seeping through cracks, she recognized the broken television, the long cobwebs hanging off the ceiling like macabre streamers.

Where is the open window?

Glass crunched under her feet. She spun about, thinking she must be mistaken.

The window was boarded up from the inside, a smaller panel fixed in place by nails. She stepped back from the closed window and felt the building close in on her. She wasn't alone. Someone was inside the room with her.

As she backed away, she fell over a broken bucket and sliced her palms on the glass-ridden floor. Her own shard fell off into the darkness. As she felt blindly for her weapon, someone laughed.

Footsteps moved toward her through the shadows.

With a scream poised at the back of her throat, she swiped her hand across the floor, sifting through grime and dust until she found the cloth-wrapped shard. Picking up the weapon, she rushed through the room, the heavy footfalls just behind.

In the hallway she ran in complete darkness. Sensing

the stairwell was close, she slowed herself and ran her hand along on the wall until she found the door. She could hear footsteps pounding through the room, boxes and machinery overturning and crashing to the floor. Silently she slipped open the stairwell door and began to climb, battling against her desperation to rush. She stepped carefully so that she made no sound, all the while terrified the door would crash open behind her.

Please be upstairs, Charlie.

She prayed he wasn't injured, hoped the madman on the first floor hadn't killed…

No.

She wouldn't allow herself to believe Charlie was dead.

One step groaned loudly under her weight. She held her breath.

The crashes ceased below her. Had he heard?

She moved faster, the need to find Charlie outweighing caution.

She was nearly to the third floor when the stairwell door groaned open behind her. She forced herself not to cry.

Rachel's hands felt for the door, and she swung it open as someone climbed the stairs. Moonlight through the door she'd opened provided enough light to guide her. She ran past the opened room, counting the doors until she found the one they'd hidden behind. The decay smell hit her like a wall, and she nearly vomited before she pulled open the door and slid inside.

Her heart sank. Charlie wasn't here.

Did I really believe he'd be waiting for me?

Locking the bolt, she ran to the broken window and looked down, hoping against hope that she'd see someone in the parking lot and finding no one.

The stairwell door squealed open.

Footsteps pounded down the corridor.

Rachel stuck her head out the window to scream for help. She stopped herself, not wanting to give herself away.

Not yet.

As she peered through cracks in the door, a large shape lumbered past and stopped. Heavy breathing filled the hallway.

She slipped beside the door, out of view in case the madman peered through one of the cracks. Her hand tightly gripped the shard of glass.

The hall went quiet. From her angle she couldn't see his shape in front of the door, yet she sensed him.

Waiting.

The rotted door would offer little resistance.

The knob turned.

Warmth trickled down her pant legs as she wet herself.

The door rattled on its hinges. A full moon with haunted eyes glared through the window as if beckoning her to leap.

The shaking stopped.

Please go away.

She pressed her back against the wall, not daring to look at the door. She heard his breathing, imagined the hulking shadow seen through the door cracks. The floor moaned under his weight.

Another door squealed open. *The door directly across?* She thought so, but the way the whole building groaned with each new sound made it difficult to tell.

Clutching the shard to her chest, ready to lash out if the door crashed open, she listened as his footfalls trailed back down the hallway. She closed her eyes and thanked her parents, thanked God, thanked anyone responsible for this miracle. After a tense moment of quiet, the stairwell door opened and banged shut.

She slumped down to her knees and wept. The shard

fell from her hands. Through the blur of tears she read nine o'clock on her watch. The police would be looking for her now. She knew the rules about filing a missing persons report, but she was a minor, it was well after dark, and her father wouldn't take no for an answer.

Somewhere off in Treman Mills a siren wailed.

I'm a needle in a haystack. Nobody knows where to look for me.

From the street, this was just another boarded-up building. With the front window blocked, there was no sign of entry or mischief.

She had no idea where the man was inside the building. Or even if he was still inside.

Who was he? It couldn't be Thorn—the man at the door was too large. Maybe one of the other Black Thorns…

No matter how strong her desire was to escape, she promised herself to stay put until fifteen minutes after nine. Fifteen minutes for the stranger to leave the building or wander up through its vacant corridors, far away from her. Fifteen minutes to convince him that the locked door on the third floor didn't hide anyone.

The day's warmth had evacuated from the lower floors and risen away from her. The chill of autumn spilled through the window; she rubbed gooseflesh off her arms. A few more degrees colder and she'd see her breath. Every few minutes debris crumbled and fell past the window, and vermin crawled inside the walls. It took silence to show her how loud the building was after dark.

Passing like hours, the minutes ticked painfully slow. She grew tired.

Rachel caught her head bobbing and jolted herself awake. She was surprised that her watch read 9:30.

Knees cracking like firecrackers, she pulled herself up and crept to the door.

Still no signs of life in the hallway.

The terrible scent awaited her at the door cracks along with a new smell—something salty and pungent. She coughed into her shirt, willing herself not to be sick.

With one hand gripping the weapon and the other covering her mouth and nose, she squinted through the holes.

The doorway across the hall stood open.

The hallway was quiet, aglimmer in the eerie blue of moonlight.

Rachel ground her teeth and quietly slid back the bolt, worrying that she'd been tricked. The stranger might never have left the floor. She'd only heard the stairwell door open and close. Maybe he'd fooled her and crept back to the door.

Holding a butcher's knife.

Her desire to escape, to survive, steeled her nerves. She pulled back the door, wincing when the hinges squealed.

She froze at the threshold. The hallway wall and floor were soaked with fresh urine, spread as though an animal had marked its territory. Glancing up and down the hallway, she stepped back from the waste.

Her eyes rose to the open doorway. A long plastic bag extended across the floor, the insides caked by a dried liquid that appeared black in the moonlight.

She didn't want to look closer. Her legs seemed to carry her into the room.

She saw.

The bag was stuffed full of body parts—a leg severed below the knee...a hand with a school ring on a finger...long, blonde hair affixed to a bloody scalp...

At the sight of the bag's contents, she regurgitated down the front of her shirt.

Five missing persons.

Something else was stuck to the plastic. Her instinct

pleaded with her to run, but somehow she knew she needed to look closer. Shielding her eyes from the gore, she bent closer to the bag.

A dried wad of gum emblazoned with a thumbprint was stuck to the bag.

In the corner of the room, shadows stirred. She screamed as Charlie rushed out of the darkness, insanity in his eyes.

An axe whistled toward her head. She lunged at the last moment as the axe tore a chunk out of the floor. His hand caught her ankle as she turned into the hallway, toppling her into the wall. Her hands sank into the urine-soaked carpet.

The air burst from her lungs as he dived onto her back, gripping her by the hair and slamming her face into the floor. The salty waste stuck to her lips. Two of her front teeth cracked, and as he ripped back on her hair, a long, bloody drool connected her mouth to the grimy carpet.

She kicked back, an act of desperation that luckily found his groin. He rolled off of her, knees drawn up to his chest, grunting like a hog with its throat slit.

The long empty hallway stretched into darkness, her escape route.

I run faster than you.

Sucking air into her lungs, she leaped off the carpet.

His hand gripped her pant leg, and she fell again.

As she scrambled back to her knees, Charlie dragged her backward.

He bit into her arm. She shrieked, feeling his teeth hook into her arm at the elbow, tearing flesh. As she tried to pull her arm free, there came a sound like egg shells cracking. She fell into the wall, squealing and clasping the two severed bones sticking out of her skin.

He crawled after her, and she limped away.

She tried not to look at the pale, bloody splinters as

she stumbled down the hall, half-crazed by pain.

She felt him coming from behind, the weight of his footfalls causing the floorboards to tremble and buckle. His hand touched her hair, and she whirled around and slashed the broken glass across his chest. The shard tore through shirt and skin, cutting a bloody river through his nipple.

Crying out, he fell back against the wall. Blood welled out from where his hand cupped his breast.

When he threw himself at her again, she tore the shard across his face, narrowly missing his eyes. As he toppled backward, she hobbled down the corridor, clutching her ruined arm. She heard him roar.

He's going back for the axe.

The hallway rolled and tumbled before her eyes. Rachel focused on keeping her legs moving as nausea and dizziness tried to pull her to the floor, down to the carpet, down to where he'd dragged five dead bodies across the floor.

The stairwell door, hidden by black pools of shadow, was just ahead. Turning her head, she saw the axe emerge from his killing room, as though the weapon itself was chasing her.

"Why are you doing this?"

He didn't answer. His eyes appeared lost, delusional. He swung the axe, and a closed door became splinters and sawdust.

The darkness of the stairwell immediately disoriented her—she tripped on the top step and nearly tumbled down —as she contemplated whether to retreat up or down the stairs.

She chose to descend. Instead of racing to the bottom floor, she quietly slipped through the second floor doorway and tiptoed into the darkness.

Stomping down the steps, he screamed her name in the stairwell. Hot blood slid out from her elbow. She wanted to pull off her shirt and wrap it around the exposed flesh and bone but knew the task would be next to impossible with one arm hanging limp. The thought of cloth or anything touching her elbow made her cringe. Slumped against a filthy wall, she held her breath until Charlie passed her floor and headed for the lowest level.

A blast of chilly air swirled out of an open doorway and into the hallway. A small circle of light like a standing pool shimmered outside the doorway, providing enough ambient light for Rachel to see. Had she missed an open window? Limping toward the open door, she felt her hope grow.

The doorway opened to a storage room, cardboard boxes stacked in the corners and along the far wall. A chunk of panel was missing from the shattered window, allowing light and a night wind to penetrate the building. The opening was large enough for her head to squeeze through but too constricted for her body.

The stairwell door opened and closed below her, and Charlie's footfalls trailed down the hall and into the old sports cards store.

The rusty fence top stood five feet below, the blacktop another six feet down.

Eleven feet.

I can survive an eleven foot drop.

Her head swam each time the wound throbbed. She didn't think she'd survive another hour without passing out.

At any moment Charlie would realize she wasn't on the first floor, and this would be the next place he'd check. She looked around desperately for a tool to pry off the panel. Opening a box, she rummaged through brittle, bug-eaten pamphlets, finding nothing useful.

It was quiet downstairs, and that unsettled Rachel. Despite how unsettling it was to hear him smashing things below, it was scarier not to know where he was.

The darkness thickened in the room.

The hair on the back of her neck stood on end.

Someone was behind her.

She swung around with the glass shard in hand and found herself looking down the barrel of a gun.

Rachel thrust the glass at her attacker. The unseen man caught her hand, twisting it until the shard fell harmlessly to the floor.

This is it. He's going to kill me.

"What the hell are you doing in here, water bug?"

When he lowered the gun, she recognized Thorn's face. Torn between relief that it wasn't Charlie and fear of what the Black Thorns were going to do to her, she backed toward the window. Moonlight illuminated a long scar running down one side of his face. A tattoo snaked from one of his eyes to the back of his shaved head.

She felt his eyes burning into her. Her throat was too parched to speak.

He saw the gory fragmentation of her elbow.

"Jesus. What happened to you?"

He leaned down to look at the wound, and she flinched away.

"Easy. I'm not gonna touch you."

Removing a hooded sweatshirt, he pulled his t-shirt over his head and folded it.

"Here," he said, handing her the shirt. "Wrap it around your elbow. Keep that wound covered."

Her lips quivered, imagining how much it would hurt to wrap cloth around the compound fracture. "I can't."

"I ain't a doctor. But if you leave that wound exposed in this dust, you'll need your arm amputated by sunrise. Now, tell me why in the hell you're hiding in Black Thorns territory after sunset. Trespassing is enough to get you killed in this part of the city."

She shot him an angry glare.

"What are you going to do to me, Thorn? Are you gonna shoot me and leave me to die in this place?"

"You know the penalty for crossing our borders." His words stung, but she noticed his eyes had softened.

"You're doing a shitty job of policing your borders. You have no idea what's going on inside this building."

A floorboard groaned below. His eyes interrogated hers.

He pointed the gun at her.

"Who else is inside the building with you?"

Rachel shook her head. "That's what I've been trying to tell you. Charlie Tanner is downstairs."

"Tanner? Why the fuck is that asshole jock sneaking around my building?" Thorn stepped forward. He pressed the cool steel barrel against her forehead. "You better give me an answer that I like, water bug, or this room is gonna get messy."

She swallowed, wondering if she should tell him the truth. Would he believe her?

He pulled back on the hammer.

"He's killing people."

She shut her eyes and waited for the gun to fire.

"What do you mean, *killing people*?"

When she opened her eyes she saw him staring at her as if she'd grown a third arm.

"It's true. You know all those missing persons stories in the newspapers? Charlie killed them."

"How do you know this?"

"I saw the bodies. They're on the third floor near the end of the hall. And now he wants to kill me."

He lowered the gun, and she felt her heart skip. He studied her skeptically, his glare moving back to her injury. Gritting her teeth, she wrapped his shirt around her punctured flesh and exposed bone. Pain tore through her elbow; tears sketched rivers down her dusty cheeks.

Never taking his eyes off her, he dug into his pocket, thumbed a number into his phone, and lifted the receiver to his ear. She heard it ringing, then a male voice answered.

"Yeah...we've got a problem up here...what floor? I think it's the—"

A guttural scream came out of the darkness. Before Rachel knew what was happening, the axe swung at Thorn's head. He ducked under the cutting edge, but the handle came back around and crushed the back of his neck.

Thorn collapsed to the floor as the phone flew out of his hand and struck the wall. She heard the voice on the other end calling out to Thorn, asking him what was happening.

"We're on the second floor! He's gonna kill us!"

Praying the other person had heard her, she screamed as the axe crushed the phone.

A torrent of blood rushed from Thorn's nose. As he started to push himself up, Charlie stomped down on the back of his head. There was a sickening crunch as Thorn's face bounced off the floor.

Charlie rounded on her, one bloody hand clasped to the slash across his breast, the other holding the axe.

"Please."

He leaped forward. She raked the glass across his face, and he screamed and fell back. A jagged crimson line formed where the shard had cut, the point having torn across the bridge of his nose and missed his eye by a fraction of an inch.

Wiping blood off his stunned face, he looked between his hand and her eyes.

He began to laugh. A block of ice formed in her chest.

When he grinned, she saw that his teeth were streaked with crimson. Looking at her cloth-wrapped elbow, he clicked his teeth together.

He pointed the axe at her. The cutting edge, marred by splintered wood and hair, was a hair's width from her face.

Rachel backed away, and he came at her. The blade whistled past her ear and exploded against the wall. When he ripped the cutting edge free of the hole, she could see into the next room.

Screaming, he raised the axe over his head. As the blade hammered down, she threw herself sideways. Board shattered as the axe head smashed through the floor. Grunting, he wrestled with the handle, the blade lodged in the floorboards.

She drove the shard into his ribcage. He reached for her, and she slashed the shard across his Adam's apple.

Charlie crumbled backward, his weight shaking the floor. He lay twitching, his legs possessed by spasms, trying to get up, trying to turn and grab her, his eyes filled with hate. A waterfall of blood rushed out from his neck. When he tried to speak, blood bubbled out of his mouth.

His arm reached across the dusty floor to where the axe rested. Then he collapsed and lay staring at the ceiling, chest heaving.

She hadn't noticed Thorn rise to his feet until he stood beside her. Holding the back of his neck, he spat down on Charlie.

The stairwell door crashed open. At the sound of footsteps racing down the hall, Thorn raised the gun and pointed it at the doorway. He lowered it upon recognizing three members of the Black Thorns. They started to ask him what had happened, but the glare he shot back at them brought silence.

Charlie coughed and sprayed blood against her pant legs.

"My God," Rachel said. "I killed someone. I killed Charlie Tanner."

Thorn met her eyes. "You were never here."

"But I—"

"I said *you were never here*." He held out an open hand. "Give me the glass."

Below their feet, Charlie sputtered and gurgled. A dark, expanding pool of blood under his neck trickled toward her shoes. With shaking hands, she gave Thorn the weapon.

"Let her pass," said Thorn, and the three Black Thorns stepped away from the doorway. They didn't speak to her, but their stares were hard as she backed toward the threshold.

Thorn pointed the gun at Charlie. As if on cue, the other members aimed their weapons at the huge boy sprawled on the floor.

She was into the hallway now, unable to tear her eyes away from the scene inside the room.

Thorn raised his head toward her. Even with the moon at his back, she could feel his eyes burning.

"Run, little water bug. Run away like a good little girl. You shouldn't be in Black Thorns territory after dark."

She turned toward the black hallway, the scent of death rolling down from the third floor.

She ran.

As she rushed down the stairs, uncaring of what dangers the darkness might hide, gunfire exploded from the second floor. Careening off walls, stumbling over boxes, she never stopped running until she climbed through the window the Black Thorns had broken into.

She spilled out onto the concrete.

The night was cold, the moon invisible behind the towering building. She stared up at those boarded windows like dead eyes, and as she crawled to her knees she heard the banshee cries of sirens off in the city. The death scent crept out through the window, following her.

Rachel knew people were still inside, yet she felt a desperate need to board up that window and keep the evil that festered inside from crawling into the night.

As she backed away, stumbling blindly over the

cracked and buckled sidewalk, she knew she was too late. The evil was already out.

One Autumn in Kane Grove

The autumn of Kane Grove was born teetering on the edge of extinction.

As the wind whistled a frigid requiem against the outer walls of the university library's computer wing, I saw myself quoted on the Internet, this time on one of those big news websites like the ones that cover presidential primaries, the Dow Jones, and Middle-Eastern wars. The quote was nebulous, and honestly I don't remember much about it, except that a mousy female reporter stuck her smart phone in my face as I was hurrying across the quad, trying to get to my calculus class before three o'clock.

Before this autumn I don't think anyone outside of New York even knew Kane Grove College existed; now you can turn on CNN and see the campus, the Jamison Sciences tower pointing into the milky sky like a fleshless finger, as harried students hustle by in the foreground.

Dad blames the university.

"This sort of thing doesn't happen at Hamilton or Bowdoin," he told me on the phone last week. "Take next semester off, and get your applications filled out. Someone as smart as you shouldn't be wasting time at a school like Kane."

Mom just sits and cries, worried sick that I'm going to be next.

On September 21st, autumn rolled into upstate New York like a January tidal wave off Nova Scotia, and campus police found the first body. As I ran up University Avenue, the sharp edges of textbooks inside my knapsack stabbing into my back, I cursed under my breath for not wearing anything heavier than a sweatshirt.

Chill and wicked, the wind whipped across the Finger Lakes like a petulant child that refused to wait for Christmas. Sunset was but an hour away, and though the hour was late and the sky a boiling mass of slate gray, I remember how much the failing light bothered my eyes, a surefire sign of a monster migraine encroaching.

A girl with her head lowered into her chest passed in the other direction, a pretty little ghost train racing to stay ahead of winter. Apparently she hadn't read or believed the weather report either because she wore cutoff jean shorts and a tank top that slouched off one shoulder. Her flip-flops slapped against the concrete to a frantic tempo that echoed staccato-like off the brick facades of bordering dormitories. It wasn't until I guiltily stole a glance at her from behind that I realized the girl was Kari Morton.

Halfway up the hill to my dormitory, Lee Hall, I scarfed down a slice of white pizza from the Bethany Union cafeteria. I hadn't eaten since breakfast, which was probably the reason I started getting a headache, and hell if I didn't want to take refuge from the biting cold for a few minutes. Big mistake. Fifteen minutes later I was hunched over and heaving something that looked like pizza into a toilet as I thought about whose ass I was going to kick for giving me food poisoning. I don't remember how I ended up in my dorm room or falling asleep on my bed.

Around ten o'clock my roommate, Mitch Hollingsworth, wearing a *Make Art Not War* t-shirt, excitedly whipped our door open, denting the plaster with an outline of the knob. To my delicate ears it sounded like a shotgun blast.

"What do you think about Kari Morton?"

"What?" The room spun as if I had just stepped off one of those playground merry-go-rounds that used to make me nauseous.

"Holy crap, Dan. What the hell is wrong with you?" I don't think Mitch was concerned about my health so much as he didn't want to catch whatever it was I had. He took a step backward.

"Food poisoning. Bad pizza. I'd stay away from

Bethany if I were you."

"That sucks, but you gotta hear this," he raced on, evidently no longer concerned about whether I might roll over and die. "Campus security found Kari Morton dead near the quad."

"Dead?"

"Murdered."

"Murdered?"

"Is there an echo in here?"

I felt like someone punched me in the teeth.

"The cops are everywhere. But that isn't the craziest part," Mitch said, and by the way he emphasized the last part I sensed it had been killing him to get to the gory details. "The guy who did it must have been a total wacko. He stabbed her in the neck."

As I thought about Kari racing past me on University Avenue, so close I could have touched her bare shoulders or breathed the mango-scented shampoo in her bouncing, brunette curls, a chill ran through my bones, like a phantom passed right through me.

"What time did this happen?"

"After dark. Probably 7:30 or 8 o'clock."

When had I passed her? Ninety minutes prior to her murder, if that.

"How do you know all of this?"

"You know Sam from chem lab? Well, he knows this dude from Randall Hall that was at the front of the police barricade when they were zipping her up."

"Zipping her up?"

"Body bag, duh."

"Yeah, right."

"Are you sure you're okay?"

"I feel like shit. I might skip psych tomorrow morning."

"Yeah, man. Sleep in. You look like spoiled yogurt. Smell like it, too."

"Up yours. Do the police know who killed her?"

"No. But Sam knows this other dude who says Kari broke up with some townie she was dating."

"Kari dated a townie?"

"I know, right? Big guy. Football player or something. Sam says he was nuts. *Freaking* nuts. But what do you expect from a gap-toothed, tobacco-spittin' townie?"

"Oh sure, everyone's hometown is backwards except for the one *you* came from," said a female voice from around the corner. Appearing in the doorway, Gina Artuso wore a concerned look on her face.

Self-consciously pulling the blanket toward my face, I felt the heat in my cheeks. God, I didn't want her to see me like this. Gina came to my bedside, curly blonde locks draped over her shoulder. "Is it the pandemic?"

"Yeah. You'll be dead by morning."

"Then I guess you aren't taking me out for pizza Friday night?"

Just hearing the word *pizza* sent my stomach roiling again.

"Just something I ate. I'll be fine tomorrow."

**

The next morning I skipped psychology and slept straight through chemistry, too. Stumbling out of bed at noon, I felt as though I had the worst hangover of my life.

Having missed my only classes of the day, I ventured out at one o'clock on legs that shook as much from disquiet as they did from food poisoning. The quad bustled with conversation. I looked at everyone a little differently, and they did the same to me.

The sun was out again, and the way that it glared off the white concrete made my head feel as if it was trapped inside a vise. Nevertheless, I fought the urge to wear sunglasses, wanting to appear as inconspicuous as possible, the way you might keep your hands out of your pockets in an unfamiliar convenience store so nobody gets the mistaken impression you are shoplifting or hiding a handgun.

Except for a few lone individuals hurrying between classes, most everyone on the quad was broken into groups which quickly formed, broke up, and reformed like transient football huddles. The rumble of conversation drifted out of the concentric gatherings, bits and pieces catching on the wind.

"...knew a guy who knew someone who dated her last year."

"...gouged out her throat."

"She was such a pretty girl. Why would someone..."

"Some asshole townie..."

Amid the disorganized groups crawled a small army of police and campus security, each faction vying for dominance over the investigation. For the next three days the cops buzzed about like worker bees, and then the university returned to normalcy, Kari's murder a baleful whisper on the wind.

A sea of charcoal-gray clouds rolled overhead during the first week of October in concert with a Lake Ontario wind that cut through double-layered sweatshirts and sweatpants and demanded we grudgingly don winter jackets. The coldest autumn air mass the northeast had seen in twenty years poured into Kane Grove.

My afternoon migraines came and went like the tide, but they became frequent enough that Mitch threw me into his car one afternoon and drove me to a nearby walk-in clinic. A graying doctor with a combination pencil-thin mustache and disheveled hairdo which made him look like a cross between Clark Gable and Albert Einstein poked and prodded me for thirty minutes. He gave me the usual rest and relaxation advice doctors give to people with head colds

71

and advanced stages of cancer. Three days later I received a voicemail from his office complaining my white count was low and I needed to eat more fruits and vegetables.

The campus buzz over Kari Morton dissipated to the occasional nervous whisper before the Kane Grove police department found the second body—a twenty-something woman in her third year of teaching at Medwick Elementary School three blocks north of campus. Her name was Maryann Neville. Reading the story in the GROVE PRESS, I shivered. I knew well the area around Medwick and often biked there when the weather was more reasonable.

I felt an overwhelming sense of deja vu as I studied her smiling face on the front page. Pulled back into a ponytail, her blonde hair had a vibrant glow that the black-and-white medium couldn't suppress. Far be it from me to forget a pretty face. Surely in a town as small as Kane Grove we had happened upon one another in a grocery store checkout line or downtown bar. Perhaps I had brushed up against her in Starbucks, our eyes meeting as her lips curled into a smile.

Miss Neville had reportedly stayed past dark to fight her way through a backlog of homework assignments. As desiccated leaves rained in variegated oranges around Miss Neville on the evening of October 4th, she rushed toward her vehicle in the deserted school parking lot. Her shoes scuffled against the concrete, and leaves crunched underfoot like the cackle of witches as the long, black fingers of lamppost shadows reached across the parking lot. She had nearly reached her blue Prius, a lifeless slate in the moonlight, when—

Her body was found at midnight by Harley Bouchard, an overnight janitor who had stepped outside for a smoke and a look at the stars. He found Neville lifelessly staring into a depthless sky, a considerable chunk missing from her neck.

Considerable debate erupted over the nature of her

wound. The police referred to it as a deep gouge, possibly from a knife or some other sharp implement, while the coroner controversially suggested the wound was more consistent with an animal attack. But the macabre debate between the police and coroner was drowned out by the holy war being waged between the town of Kane Grove and its university.

Hysterical and dripping with vigilantism, commentary in the town's GROVE PRESS purported the Neville murder was retaliation by university students for the murder of Kari Morton. Some called for the university to be closed indefinitely until the murderer was rooted out. The argument seemed shallow since there were no suspects in the Morton murder, despite water cooler talk of the psychotic townie boyfriend.

There is a thicket on campus that stretches from the hill dormitories at the top of University Avenue down past the backside of the buildings along the northern border of the quad. Buckled into humps by subterranean tree roots and brutally long winters, a blacktop walkway side winds through the thicket down to Branson Creek Road. The thicket path is a preferred route for most students, as it provides a shortcut to both the quad and to two convenience stores just north of campus.

By the end of the first week of October, the path through the thicket developed a sense of foreboding, as though a great weight pushed down on it. I had just come from the store on a Monday evening, and as I climbed the path the wind dirged through the tree tops. I huddled against the bitter wind that seemed determined to force its way inside of me.

Skeletal trees rose black all around me, with still a few dried leaf carcasses left to drift earthward. I jumped each time I heard tree limbs rubbing against each other, sounding as though saws were cutting through bone. I quickened my pace, expecting something to jump out at me from the trees.

Heart racing, I emerged to ashen parking lot lamplight behind the Jamison Sciences tower. I hurried forward without looking back, feeling as if I had escaped a haunted house

When I entered the student center in the heart of the quad, a black, boiling cauldron of hysteria overtook the students. I learned from one breathless girl that Kari Morton's body had been stolen from Pineview Cemetery in her hometown outside of Syracuse. Some students supported the notion that townies were responsible.

The idea that a vigilante group of Kane Grove citizens had driven forty miles to desecrate a teenage girl's gravesite was preposterous; but it didn't quell the coming week's vandalism and fistfights spreading through Kane Grove like air rippling outward from a bomb blast.

**

Though my headaches lessened into mid-October, my sleep became more fitful. When I dreamed, I often found myself within the thicket, the gnarled limbs of barren trees reaching toward me, the bitter wind the screams of Kari Morton and Maryann Neville.

After the third body, a sensual, redheaded university junior named Laila Jennings, was discovered by a campus security patrolman a week before Halloween, Kane Grove College descended into panic. While some of us had known the Morton girl, and none had much idea who the teacher from town was, everyone had known Laila.

She was known as Three Degrees of Laila, for if you didn't know someone who knew someone who had had intimate relations with her, you apparently didn't get out very much. I sat behind her in modern poetry class last spring, my eyes always following along the curves of her smooth legs and searching down low-cut shirts whenever she bent to retrieve her book bag.

The campus cop who found her had been walking along the shadowed walkway between the five-story library and the student center, his flashlight beam cutting across the pallid concrete in erratic, nervous sweeps. The beam happened upon a heel on the edge of the sidewalk, and as he gasped, the light found Laila, legs akimbo, body splayed in the grass at the base of the student center ten yards from the shoe. A large chunk of flesh was missing from the right side of her neck.

The next morning we were double-barrel blasted by two rumors which swept through the university. This time the police agreed with the coroner—the gaping hole in the side of Laila's neck was more consistent with an animal attack than that made by a weapon. No sooner did this piece of news begin to make its rounds than we learned the body of Maryann Neville had vanished from a cemetery near Albany.

It didn't take long for the more imaginative and delirious among us to suggest the attacks were not those of man or animal but rather of supernatural origin. Perhaps the bodies were not disappearing from grave sites but were leaving on their own.

The word *vampire* was probably first whispered over lattes and bagels at the student center. Promulgating like a disease, the concept spread through email and over too many drinks at the bars until it became accepted fact that Nosferatu walked among us.

Feeding off the hysteria, every media faction—from local reporters to occult bloggers and national news outlets —swooped down upon us like hungry grackles two days prior to Halloween. That was the same day the female reporter wrestled an incongruous quote from me as I rushed to class. I am certain, quite certain, I had scoffed at the idea of the killer being a vampire. Yet somehow a modernized and bizarre version of the telephone game ensued, and my quote morphed through several iterations, until a national news website had me purporting that Bela Lugosi was running amok.

It was not my parents' proudest moment.

By now Mom and Dad started leaving me daily voicemails of their intentions to drive to Kane Grove and bring me home. But I couldn't leave. As frightened as I was, the frenzy attracted me, the way rubberneckers slow down on the highway to watch the bodies being removed from a wreck. Besides, things were starting to progress between Gina and me, and I wasn't about to leave her alone on campus with a psycho killer.

My roommate, Mitch, got roughed up one night outside of the One For The Road Tavern—a favorite among townies—when three unknown men yanked him out of the passenger seat of an idling vehicle. Mostly they just shoved Mitch among the three of them, like an old pinball machine where the obstacles light up and hurl the ball at a random diagonal, telling Mitch to spread the word that university pricks weren't welcome downtown anymore.

Gina and I picked up Mitch, and as we drove back toward campus, a blur of streetlights and mostly darkened residences whirring past to either side of Harper Hill, he began to smirk over the assumption that a vampire was loose in Kane Grove.

"But if it really *is* a vampire," he said, "it won't be hard to figure out who he is."

"How do you mean?" Gina asked, eyeing him in the rearview mirror as she drove.

"Well, he can't come out in daylight. Who do we know who sleeps all day? I'm thinking it must be one of the townie night shift janitors."

"You watch too many movies."

"And you blame everything on townies," I said.

Gina said, "Just because Dracula had to sleep in a coffin all day doesn't mean a real vampire needs to avoid the sun."

"She's right," I said. "You can never trust Hollywood.

For all we know, he drinks holy water and listens to Gregorian chants while he builds up his vampire skills at the gym."

Mitch laughed, and then he leaned forward from the back seat and said, "Well, I for one suggest we all keep a stake handy and line our windowpanes with garlic."

**

My headaches continued to ebb and flow through October. Finally, whatever illness that had ailed me since the first day of autumn fled my body on the day before Halloween, when I vomited on the steps outside of the interfaith chapel. Gina was with me, and as the crowd backed away from us as though I could kill by touch, Gina wrestled me toward her car, demanding I return to the walk-in clinic. No sooner had we reached the vehicle than the color returned to my cheeks.

"Don't even start with that *it must have been something I ate* bullcrap," she said.

"I'm okay now. Actually I feel pretty damn great," I said.

And I did. Suddenly I felt as though I had had the best night of sleep of my life. I possessed an incredible sense of clarity, and I felt the muscles in my arms standing out like cords beneath my shirt. I'm not exaggerating when I say that calculus derivations swam through my mind. I didn't have any explanation as to why I had so much energy, but if Gina had dropped me off at the gym, I think I could have lifted twice my weight over my head.

Studying my face, perplexed, she said, "You do look better, I suppose."

"You don't look like such a slouch, yourself," I said, and she punched me in the arm.

But as she drove us back toward Lee Hall above University Avenue between curbside mountains of raked leaves which caught the sun in varied shades of ocher, I warily eyed the dashboard clock.

Noon.

Less than six hours until sunset.

I walked Gina to her room on the girls' floor, two levels below ours, and she kissed me long on the lips at her door. That afternoon, despite feeling healthier than I had since summer, I fell asleep watching football in my dorm room. Devoid of dreams, my slumber was at once the sleep of the dead and strangely revitalizing. With Mitch away for the weekend, I might have slept clear through the night had I not awakened to shouts ringing through the dormitory hallway.

I bolted upright, unsure of where I was. The room was dark except for the television replaying highlights of the games I missed. My bedside alarm clock glowed 10:38.

When I poked my head into the hallway, the corridor started filling with students. They wore haunted expressions on their faces as I closed the door behind me, and when I started to ask the closest person what had happened, a cold dread pouring down my back, Gina pushed her way through the crowd to reach me.

"What the heck is going on?" I asked her. Gina's eyes were wide and distant as though she were seeing an alternate reality through the wall behind me.

"They found another body, Dan. This time...it's horrible." Her lips began to quiver, and I pulled her against me. Her hands sought the folds in my sweatshirt, chest heaving as she sobbed. "They are going to have to close the school."

"Nobody's going to close the school," I said, caressing her hair. "Do you know how much money the university and town would lose if Kane shut its doors?"

"I don't care if they shut Kane down forever. It could have been one of us this time. It could have been..."

The girl was Kelly Dillon. I realized with building horror

that not only had she lived in Lee Hall three doors down from Gina, but that I once dated her for a short time last year. Too close to home.

I was not surprised to learn Kelly had been found in the thicket behind Jamison. A couple walking through the thicket, holding hands and watching the swaying trees uneasily, were surprised by what they thought were raindrops. But the droplets were too viscid and dark to be rain. When they looked up through the trees toward the wind-torn sky and the screaming face of a full moon creeping out from behind the clouds, they saw Kelly.

She was suspended a hundred feet off the ground, her arms outstretched and tied to two bordering limbs. Grotesquely lolled to the side, her neck oozed a steady leakage of ichor. The couple, thinking they had walked through a mud puddle, suddenly realized what they were standing in, and the girl began to scream uncontrollably.

The left side of Kelly Dillion's neck was...missing, as though some beast had crashed through the thicket and ripped it away with razors for fangs. The wind became a shrill force. The girl saw the shadows move from over her boyfriend's shoulder. She became inconsolable, trying to warn the boy that someone was in the thicket with them, but she was unable to form words. And all about the couple, as the skeletal silhouettes of trees swayed as though laughing, Kelly continued to drip...drip...drip...

It took half the night for police to retrieve the body from the tree tops. It must have been the oddest of crime scene investigations, and I could not help but muse with a wry humor that only seems attainable in the midst of absolute terror, how they would have solved this murder on one of those reality TV cop shows.

The next day—Halloween Day—the university president, Dr. Branson Horwith, waffled uneasily during a televised press conference. Sweat beaded and ran in rivulets across his beet-red face. Most students didn't wait for Horwith's decision to keep the university open or close it down, choosing instead to depart Kane Grove as the sun reached its apex and began its inevitable descent toward the horizon.

Riots spread through Kane Grove that afternoon, though I am not convinced the remaining students or town citizens knew what they were fighting over. Gina wanted to leave but found her tires slashed in the dormitory parking lot. Her parents were coming to get her, but they would not arrive from Maryland until the following morning. Only five people remained in Lee Hall on our floor.

Gina fell asleep on my bed around 5:30. Already the shadows grew long on the walkways leading toward the quad. I watched with trepidation as the bloody orb of the dying sun was dragged toward the horizon. I had a commanding view of the valley. Sweeping across the horizon, my eyes centered on an odd procession: a miniature parade of garish costumes, flashlights, and shades of orange. Trick-or-treaters, rushing to embrace the holiday before the unseen dangers of nightfall reached Kane Grove.

I gently shook Gina's shoulder and said, "I need to eat. I'm starving."

She muttered something about being careful and getting back before sunset.

"I'll be back. I promise."

I brushed her hair away and kissed her on the forehead. Glancing one last time out the window, I saw the sun appear to accelerate toward the earth as though dragged into an open grave.

**

Jesus, it was cold. As I raced against time toward the thicket pathway, I pulled the hood of my sweatshirt over my head and yanked tight on the drawstrings. Save for three tightly-grouped students walking in the distance, the university sidewalks appeared deserted. Incandescent lighting shone through a wide scattering of windows, peering at me like cat's eyes.

A haunted wind moaned through the trees, and as the already blackened thicket pathway came into view behind Jamison, I knew the sun would surely set by the time I returned from the convenience store.

The trees seemed taller in the failing light, leering down at me as I strode into the heart of the thicket. Dead leaves crackled underfoot like brittle bones. All I heard was the unsettling song of the wind through the trees and the sound of footfalls. Were the footfalls mine, or were there others behind me? Sounds have a funny way of echoing off the trees in the thicket. I glanced behind uneasily. Shadows reached across the pathway, swimming with movement.

At the center of the thicket, just off the pathway, stood a rickety, wooden maintenance shed. I never liked passing the old shed during the daytime, and as I moved past it with nightfall rapidly invading, my eyes were drawn to it as Hansel's and Gretel's surely had been to the witch's lair.

Movement in the shed's window caught my eye. A face. Something. It could have been my reflection...it could have...

Overcome by blood rushing into my head, I collapsed to the earth. My head throbbed, pounded, feeling as though it might burst. I vaguely recall wishing the Gable-Einstein doctor had been a bit more thorough before I drifted into unconsciousness.

**

Someone screamed. A woman...I think...yes it had been...

I awoke in the thicket to pitch dark, the maintenance shed no longer in front of me. Echoing through the trees, the

81

scream jolted me back to clarity, but the shrill echo drifted on the periphery of the howling wind, and I wasn't certain if the scream emanated from the thicket interior or from dream.

All about me wafted the smell of decaying leaves and the sweet scent of a wood stove from somewhere in town. I felt a rock stabbing into my back, and as I rolled onto my side, a tree root dug into my ribs.

The leaves glistened a peculiar black, shiny and sticky. Something else was in the leaves at the edge of the gloom…

maybe a rock…

no…

a shoe?

Heart thudding, I pushed myself onto hands and knees, trying to get my bearings. Behind me, I saw the faraway lights of the Jamison Sciences tower.

As the moonlight slanted through the trees, I raised my wristwatch toward my face and squinted my eyes. 11:49. My God...Gina...I had been asleep for…

The rustling of tree limbs in the inky darkness got me scrambling to my feet, and I raced diagonally down a leaf-strewn slope until I reached the pathway again. I ran for the lamplights of the parking lot, running to rid myself of the thicket, running from a building horror which slammed against my body and chilled me to the bone. I crashed out of the thicket, hearing a woman yelp in surprise as she threw the tower's back door shut. The tower lights raced past me in indistinct blurs.

When I burst into the quad, my sneakers echoing hollow off the pavement, I saw Lee Hall above University Avenue. Something drove me forward: the boundless energy I had felt the prior morning and an unrelenting terror which I knew I could not outrun.

Passing the glass entranceway to the Freeman Social Sciences building, I heard the crackle of a radio as a figure darted toward me out of the shadows dressed in a suit which marked him as some sort of federal agent. His eyes widened when he saw my face. His reaction was not surprise but utter horror. I saw only his reflection in the glass as I raced past him.

Frantic voices rang out from somewhere behind me as the lights to Lee Hall loomed closer.

Gina...please, no...

After I cut through a maze of smaller dormitories, the yelling faded into the night. Now I only heard the blood thrum inside my ears, my footfalls strangely silent on the pavement as though I were dreaming.

Lee Hall stood before me, the cold October night pouring off its concrete walls.

I stared at the cutout Halloween decorations in the entranceway, and as my eyes drifted up the dormitory's exterior, I froze. A scattering of lit windows shone orange into the gloom. In four of those windows were faces.

Kari Morton's hateful eyes gazed at me from the fourth floor.

Maryann Neville glared accusingly from the second floor.

Her eyes burning bloody red, Laila Jennings peered out from the third floor.

And from the first floor, Kelly Dillon's mouth gaped open to reveal wicked fangs.

Overcome by fear, I blinked, and then the faces were gone. Left behind was a bottomless sorrow which threatened to pull me through the earth and into its abyss. I sank to my knees, shoulders heaving as I wept in the lonesome moonlight.

"I'm sorry," I cried. "I never meant to..."

As the Halloween wind shrieked up the hill and tree limbs rustled like skittering spiders, my eyes caught movement.

Raising my head, I saw Gina, within my top floor dormitory room, slumped over and sobbing into her hands. I wanted to call out to her, to let her know she need not worry. As promised, I had returned to her. For nothing could harm me in the October moonlight.

My legs seemed to move on their own accord, carrying me toward the entranceway. Hinges squealed like vermin as I pressed the door open. I crossed the glass without casting reflection or shadow.

I climbed the stairs, footfalls echoing off the barren walls like thunder.

"I'm coming, Gina."

The Island

Read on for an excerpt

From

Dark Vanishings: Episode One

"[Dark Vanishings] will be leaving its serialized footprint all over the subgenre, making Padavona a well-known name in post-apocalyptic horror." - Horror Novel Reviews

In the gold-and-flaxen late afternoon sun, cumulus clouds threw cottony shadows against the land, and the park unwound in a lord's ransom of jade and ruby.

Where am I?

Tori awakened to the thick scent of cut grass. Bleary-eyed, she raised herself up onto her elbows and examined her surroundings. Her mountain bike dozed on its side like a sleeping lion. Fifty yards ahead was a blacktop parking lot dotted by three cars. Behind her bicycle, the grass tunneled down between bordering elm rows and sprawling blackberry bushes embellished with white flowers.

She remembered biking to the park after lunch. But had she stopped to rest? She didn't recall.

She *did* remember promising her mother to be home by three so she could shower and make it to the hairdresser by five. Ted Harrison was picking her up at seven for dinner before the high school prom, which gave her just enough time after her hair appointment to slip into her dress and—

I am so freaking late. Mom is going to kill me.

Her red, shoulder-length locks, ablaze in the late day sunshine, were littered with bits of grass and leaves. She thought of Rip Van Winkle and a beard which grew for years and years while life passed him by. How could she have slept for four hours in the town park? Hadn't the park been crowded with picnickers and fishing boats when she had biked in after lunch?

Within the desolation of the park, she felt strangely exposed.

What if Jacob had come for me while I was asleep?

Jacob Mann, the boy from third period study hall who stared at her daily with a twisted grin that never touched his slate-gray eyes. Jacob Mann, who she had seen last summer, standing among bed sheets hung to dry in her backyard, watching her through her bedroom window. Jacob Mann, who was permanently expelled for threatening Mr. Gilder, the school guidance counselor, with a switchblade.

Last December she had volunteered to distribute food at the Red Oak homeless shelter, and he had been there, standing across the street among leafless deciduous trees, winter cloak billowing like a vampire's cape, his dead stare burning holes in her.

And last month, when the ground had thawed and the community garden had become ready for planting, she had looked up from her trowel, over the rows of leafy greens, to see him watching her from the sidewalk. Crow-black hair matted to his forehead. Those lifeless eyes. That grin: at-once, vacant and baleful.

Feeling eyes upon her, she sprang to her feet. The copse of elms bordering the decline swayed to the lake breeze, and as dappled light danced amid the branches, she thought she saw a pallid face watching her from the trees.

Jacob?

Her heart thundering, she turned her head toward the bike. If Jacob burst from the trees, would she be able to pedal her way to the parking lot before he cut her off?

When she turned back, the face was gone. Shadows ran deep within the copse, as though night was pooled within, waiting for the sun to depart. But there was no deranged stalker watching her, and she began to feel a little embarrassed for letting her imagination get the best of her.

Feeling along the back pocket of her cutoff jean

shorts, she pulled out her phone and checked the time.

4:51 p.m.

She still had time to make the hair appointment.

As she ran to her bike, her shadow followed her, stretching as though it was reflected in a fun house mirror. Clutching the phone, she double-clicked her mother's smiling face. After a burst of dial tones, the phone began to ring. And ring. No answer. Stuffing the phone back into her pocket, she pedaled across the bumpy grass and hopped the bike onto the blacktop, picking up speed.

She whipped past a black Volvo—unoccupied—and accelerated across the lot, catching a glimpse of an empty red Honda Civic. The lot branched out to a winding, tree-lined park access road. She leaned to the left, taking a blind turn without checking first for traffic. Her heart pounded, and she expected to hear a car horn blare before the metal grille crushed her from the side. But the road was empty of traffic, and there was only the leafy-green smell of summer's approach on the air as she rushed toward the town center.

Below the shoulder-less two-lane, the land dropped away from a rocky cliff to a gurgling brook thirty feet below. The rear tire caught the edge of the pavement, and as the bicycle wobbled, she leaned hard to the left, righting her balance.

Two minutes later she left the access road behind and coasted into Red Oak proper, past the town courthouse and village green. Catching her breath, she pedaled harder.

4:55 p.m.

As Tori veered north onto Main Street, the modest three blocks of the town center came into view. She passed the police station on her right. Set off to her left was Bob and Mary's 24-hour diner, the gray, aluminum-sided rectangle flying past in an indistinct blur as her legs pumped faster. Beyond the diner, a half-mile west, meandered the sparkling waters of Cayuga Lake.

A landscaped island divided Main Street with parking

spaces aligned diagonally against the island and along the sides of the street. Though the spaces were choked with vehicles, Tori never saw their red brake lights flare to life. In fact, there didn't seem to be a single car moving along the street.

At the center of downtown, on Main Street's east side, stood Barbara's Boutique—a red, brick-faced square squashed between a florist and the Red Oak Cafe. Squeezing the brakes, she wiggled the bike between two SUV's and hopped the curb onto the empty sidewalk.

That was the moment when she started to worry. *Where is everyone?* Downtown was resplendent with potted flowers and cardinal splashes of low-angle sunshine. On such a warm Saturday in the upstate New York village, the street should have been busy with pre-Memorial Day shoppers and people going out for an early dinner. But there wasn't anyone to be seen despite the rows and rows of cars up and down Main Street. She half-suspected that everyone was hidden inside the shops, waiting to jump out in unison and yell *Surprise!* as if part of a "Twilight Zone"-inspired version of "Candid Camera."

Leaning the bike against a maple tree which spread a blanket of shade across the sidewalk, Tori ran up the steps. Her heart sank at the sight of the empty boutique. The boutique never closed its doors early on prom night, yet the interior was vacant.

Tori grasped the door handle and pulled, expecting to find the boutique locked. She was surprised when the door opened and the chill of air conditioning spilled down her legs.

Black leather swivel chairs were aligned along the mirrored walls. As she stepped past the cash register into the heart of the boutique, she had the impression of walking through a graveyard. Her reflection paced her on both sides of the elongated room, following her like twin phantoms.

"Hello?"

Her voice reverberated hollow against the walls.

"Mrs. Donnelly? It's Tori Daniels. I have a five o'clock appointment?"

Barbara Donnelly did not answer because Barbara Donnelly was not there. Yet the lights were on, the air conditioner was rattling through the ceiling vents, and the front door was unlocked. Anybody could have walked through the doors and cracked open the cash register.

"She probably just stepped out for a moment. Maybe I should wait for a few minutes," Tori said to herself. She sat upon one of the swivel chairs at the back of the store, idly spinning back and forth as her doppelgangers watched from the mirrors. The cool air felt nice on her skin.

Pulling her phone out of her pocket, she dialed her mother again. The phone went on ringing.

"I know you're there, Mom. Pick up. Please."

Apparently Cheryl Daniels lay hunkered down with the rest of the townsfolk, playing their little game of hide-and-go-seek on Tori. She nervously scrolled through her messages and noticed no one had written her for several hours. Several text messages had arrived during lunch hour, the last a 12:30 p.m. note from Jana Davies, suggesting that Tori and Ted meet up with Jana and her boyfriend after dinner. Since then, nothing. No missed calls. No frantic voice mails from her mother wondering where Tori was.

Is the network down?

The cooling system whispered white noise. Beyond the front door, shadows grew longer along Main Street, spilling off cars and trees like black ink.

She glanced at a set of black double doors at the back of the store. The supply room. It occurred to her that anyone could be waiting behind those doors, watching her through the slit. She felt her skin prickle.

"Mrs. Donnelly? Are you back there?"

The double doors watched her. The cooling system clanged and bucked as though something was stuck in the pipes. Suddenly the elongated store felt like a crypt, the swivel chairs like torture devices in which scissors sliced and curling irons burned. Tori pushed herself up from the chair.

The knobs to the double doors rattled behind her. Surely her imagination was playing tricks on her and she actually heard the pipes expanding and contracting, as the air conditioner pumped polar air against the afternoon heat. Tori walked straight toward the front doors. Between the swivel chairs. Past the combs and brushes set in jars of blue liquid like preserved body parts. She didn't dare look back. Because if she did, those black doors would creak open, and something unspeakable would stalk out of the darkness, running its claws along the backs of the swivel chairs as its maw opened to reveal rows of blood-soaked fangs.

No matter how fast she walked, the exit door never seemed to draw closer, as though she were walking on a treadmill. The pipes shook harder. Neglected hinges creaked behind her—the sound of the black doors inching open.

Tori ran for the front door, pulling when she should have pushed. The impact rattled the plate glass, resounding as though a kettle drum had been struck. In her panic, she thought she was locked inside the boutique. Her head cleared. She pushed through the front door and ran for the mountain bike.

The warm air felt stifling after the chill of the boutique. She threw her leg over the bike seat and pumped the pedals, racing northward past empty vehicles neatly aligned along Main Street. The streets were devoid of people. Her hair appointment and the prom long forgotten, she pedaled toward her house. As the hour passed six o'clock, Tori did not yet feel her world tearing apart at the seams. But she would. Soon.

When the police car bounced off a parked pickup truck and ramped the curb, Viper bolted awake. His eyes opened in time to see the trunk of a maple tree becoming unsettlingly large in the front windshield. The police car veered left as the side view mirror exploded against the trunk.

As the car passed under the leafy boughs of the tree, flecks of afternoon sunlight drifted across the windshield in a confused assemblage of light and dark. The car barreled through a hedge and came to a stop five feet from the brick wall of a dentist's office.

Viper glanced out the side window and saw a large, smiling tooth with legs. The tooth, wearing a Kansas City Royal's baseball cap and cleats, proclaimed—

"Brush everyday and keep the cavity monster away."

"Well, that's just fucking great. You nearly ran over a goddamn cavity fighting tooth. I'll bet you boys got your drivers licenses from one of Sally Struthers' correspondence courses."

But the two cops that had been in the front seat when Viper had dozed off were nowhere to be seen. Unless the cops crouched down beneath the seat backs, snickering about the fast one they pulled on Viper, someone owed him an explanation. The engine hummed, idling stupidly, awaiting its next orders.

"What in the wide, wide world of sports just happened?"

Viper, who was really Charles Sanderson—anyone who called him Charles got a value meal smackdown and a side of whoopass fries—tried to reason through the conundrum of a police car bounding down a city street with nobody at the wheel.

Did the two cops bail from the vehicle?

Viper felt a tinge of panic. The only plausible reason for two officers of the law to leap out of a moving vehicle was their car was about to explode. Wouldn't that put a glorious point on the afternoon?

The police had cuffed his hands behind the small of his back, and now the steel dug grooves into his wrists. A black mesh cage separated the front and back compartments of the vehicle. Craning his neck over the front seat backs, he read 4:45 p.m. on the digital dashboard clock. One of those pitiful pop country songs played on the radio. Viper would have kicked a hole in the stereo system if he could have gotten past the cage. The air conditioning had somehow gotten set to 56 degrees during the accident, and cold, stale air blew from the vents, raising goosebumps on his skin.

If the cops bailed, where are they now? Since several minutes had passed without the car bursting into flames, it was obvious there was no danger of the vehicle exploding. But why didn't he hear approaching sirens? Why didn't anyone seem to give a crap that a police car had careened off a truck and landed next to a giant tooth?

He hadn't expected the dentist to storm out of the office to find out what happened. It was a Saturday afternoon, and the good doctor was probably on the 18th green by now, completely unaware that his front hedges were flattened, and an abandoned police car was five feet from rolling through his office waiting room.

But surely someone had seen. *It's sorta hard to miss a runaway police vehicle clipping trucks and blasting over landscaping.*

And that was what was so strange to Viper. Where were the looky-loos with their mobile phone cameras? Why wasn't his picture already trending on Twitter? Looking out the back window, he saw a decided absence of people and no vehicles moving on the street. A car alarm blared up the road like a wailing infant, but that was the only sound he heard over the purr of the police car engine. No lawn mowers buzzing distant, no impatient car horns. Nothing but the susurrus of wind through the trees.

The silence of the outside world grew more acute, as if the absence of sound had become a gelatinous, fleshy entity that squished against the police car.

He cracked his neck and began to ponder how to get out of this mess. There were no door handles for backseat passengers in police cars. Imagine that. No power window controls so that a prisoner could enjoy a fresh breeze on the way to the pokey. He could forget trying to kick out the glass or the metal caging.

His reflection stared back at him in the rear view mirror: clean-shaven head, goatee, and sky blue eyes that chilled.

It's time to get out of Dodge.

Then he did something that nobody would have believed possible of a man with country muscles. Bringing his knees up to his chest, he planted his boots against the seat cushion, bent backward, and slid his cuffed hands behind his thighs. He rolled backward and slipped his legs through his arms until his hands were in his lap.

"Don't try this at home, kids," he said, leaning against the driver side back door. "This is some real David Copperfield shit."

The gap between the front seat caging and the door was just wide enough for him to wiggle his hands through. The cuffs caught on the leather seat, and there was a ripping sound as he forced his hands through the gap, tearing the leather. He stretched his fingers toward the power window controls just inches beyond his reach. A skinny punk would have been home free by now, but Viper's forearms couldn't wedge their way through the gap between seat and door.

"Goddamn."

Straining, he pushed his shoulder into the seat back. The seat inched forward, and for a brief moment his fingers touched the cool surface of the side panel. But the window controls were still a fraction of an inch away. He rested for several seconds, and when he was ready, he threw his shoulder into the seat back. The seat bucked forward, and Viper jammed his boots against the backseat. His neck muscles stood out in cords, his face flushed red, every vein displayed on his body like a relief map of river-laden terrain. His fingers stretched and stretched, touching the control panel, extending toward the controls. His right shoulder screamed, and he was sure it was going to pop out of socket.

His fingertips met the controls, and the back driver side window rolled down with an electric whine. Warm May air rolled into the car, replacing the air conditioning with the sweet smells of springtime in Missouri.

He lay against the seat, his shoulder throbbing. The clock was ticking down until emergency crews arrived, but he had the odd sensation that he had all the time in the world. As gulf air blew through the open window, the morning's timeline replayed in his head.

Five hours earlier he was parked outside Davey's Bar and Grill, a dive off of Route 65 outside of Aldritch. The morning had been a hot one, and while the faded wooden fronting of the bar reflected as twins on the lenses of his sunglasses, he had watched Buddy Loman amble his monstrous frame up the steps into the dark void beyond the bar's front door. Creedence Clearwater Revival hit Viper's pickup with a wall of sound, thumping out "Born on the Bayou." The door closed, and the music became muted. John Fogerty seemed to be singing from under a couch.

Collecting bounties was a tough lot in any economy. But this one, as they say, was *on the house*. Loman, who had been on the run for nearly two weeks, had beat the hell out of his wife in Goodland, Kansas, leaving her in a coma as a parting gift to ten years of boozing and terror. That had been just a little too close to home for Viper, who still fell asleep to a fantasy of tossing his own old man through walls for all the times he had struck Viper's mother. Dick Sanderson had taken the easy way out, choosing fatal cirrhosis over the pain that Viper would have laid upon him as an adult. And surely Dick had seen his son coming for him even at the age of twelve, those cold, blue eyes biding their time, waiting, planning.

And now there was Loman, six foot eight inches and 300 pounds of black-bearded jackass, probably lumbering up to the bar for a beer while his wife was hooked to a life support machine in Goodland.

"Time has come," Viper said, stepping onto the sun-beaten blacktop.

Walking out of the Missouri sun into the bleakness of the bar, Viper could only see the garish lights of the jukebox against the far wall and the bar counter top, which glowed in the reflected sunlight caught off the mirror behind the bar. The vague rectangular outline of a pool table near the back of the bar. A vintage cash register behind the counter which had probably been here when the bad guys rode into town on horseback.

He couldn't see Buddy, only the shadowed outlines of five men at the bar, bent over mugs. Creedence finished, segueing into the eight hi-hat shots that exploded into AC/DC's "Back in Black."

"Can I get you something?" the barkeep asked, watching Viper out of the corners of his eyes.

Viper prided himself on not being seen until he made a move on someone. But Buddy Loman had sensed eyes on his back all the way through Oklahoma and Missouri, and so he noticed that the rusty Chevy pickup in front of the bar was the same one parked across the street from his motel room last night. Buddy didn't walk up to the counter upon entering. Instead he made a sharp turn to the right as soon as he safely merged with the bar's gloom, his back pressed up against the wood paneled walls, waiting to see who was going to walk through that door.

The behemoth of a man came from behind Viper, fists balled and knuckles white.

But Viper wasn't one of the most feared bounty hunters in the central and southern plains by chance. Behind the muscle and swagger was observation and attention to detail. Even before his eyes adjusted to the darkness, he perceived that none of the men at the bar looked close to Buddy's size. His quarry must have hidden behind him. Viper was ready when the floorboards creaked.

"Looking for someone, boy?"

Viper spun around as Buddy swung. Viper ducked under the blow, feeling the breeze of Buddy's sizable fist whistling over his head. With Buddy exposed, Viper landed an uppercut to his ribs. The big man stumbled two steps backward, a mix of shock and anger in his eyes.

The shock vanishing, Buddy Loman charged Viper like a rampaging bull. "You're a dead man."

Viper sidestepped the attack and landed three blows to Buddy's back in rapid succession. Buddy fell into the bar, and the two men who were seated at those stools dove into the patrons to either side, spilling beer and popcorn.

"Time has come," Viper said as Buddy spun to face him.

"I ain't going to jail, and you ain't man enough to bring me in." Buddy balled his right fist, pulling his arm back as he prepared to deliver a roundhouse punch that would knock this bald-headed wise ass into next week. But Viper dodged the blow and countered with three quick jabs that caught Buddy's nose flush. The first blow broke the nose. The next two turned the nose into a red pulp of meat fresh from the grinder.

"I don't think you understand, Buddy. I don't aim to take you to jail. I intend to whoop your candy ass from one end of this bar to the other and let the cops peel you off the floor with a spatula."

A bloody waterfall poured from what was left of

Buddy's nose. When he tried to curse at Viper, it came out as something like, "Ruck Ooh."

Nose or not, Buddy wasn't about to back down. He lunged at Viper, bellowing like an injured elephant. Viper lowered his shoulder, and Buddy flipped over the top of him, crashing back first onto the pool table. The pool stick snapped. Three balls fell off the table and rolled toward opposite walls as though fleeing.

"You know, Buddy," Viper said, standing beside the pool table where Buddy was outstretched. "You really shouldn't have put your old lady in the hospital." Buddy's eyes rolled in his head, unfocused, as though his head was weighted down by bags of wet sand.

"She had it comin'", Buddy said, spitting out a piece of molar.

Grabbing a second pool stick, Viper called his shot. "Jackass. Corner pocket." He cracked the stick over Buddy's chest.

Buddy screamed. "You know how it is. Fuckin' whores. You gotta put 'em in their place," Buddy said, wincing.

Viper saw red. The bloodied monster on the pool table became Dick Sanderson, and it was Viper's mother laid up in a coma in Goodland. A switch flipped inside Viper's head, and Buddy saw the those cold eyes wavering between controlled rage and madness, as though Viper was a grenade with the pin pulled. That made Buddy very frightened.

Viper grasped Buddy by the shirt collar, pulling him forward with his left hand while his right fist rained punches down on Buddy's face. Buddy's eyes kept rolling around in his head. The monster on the pool table lost consciousness, hanging limp like an oversized stuffed animal.

The bartender's voice, begging Viper to stop before he killed Buddy, seemed far away, blending with the rock and roll roaring out from the jukebox.

Two silhouettes rushed out of the harsh Missouri

sunshine into the bar. As Viper pulled his fist back to deliver another blow to Buddy's purpled face, he felt his body cramp. An instant later he had the sensation of someone cracking a two-by-four across his back, and then he lay twitching on the floor as two cops holding Tasers stood over him, looking as though they had just bagged a fifty-point buck or reeled in the Loch Ness Monster.

"What the hell do we have here?" asked a tall, thin cop with reflective sunglasses that were quite unnecessary inside Davey's. He carried a look of arrogance, and as he turned to his wide-eyed partner, a pudgy fellow with a boyish face, he said, "He looks like one of them ultimate fighter types.

"Hey, junior. You hearing me down there?"

Viper's eyes turned glassy. His whole body trembled. The blurry images of the cops had doubled.

The thin cop kicked Viper in the ribs as his partner looked nervously away. "You chose the wrong town to beat somebody to death in a bar fight. But I gotta say, you got spunk…well, you *had* spunk. Wait until the boys down at the station get a load of you."

They turned Viper over, cuffed his wrists behind his back, and yanked him to his feet. Viper couldn't control his legs yet, and the two cops had to drag him out of the bar, down the steps, and into the car. A third cop buzzed past to deal with the remains of Buddy Loman, whose unconscious body hogged the pool table.

"Hell yes, we hooked a big one," the thin cop said, starting the police car engine. The vehicle pulled out of the parking lot onto the loose stone road that led back into town, kicking up rocks that pinged against the underside of the police car like a calypso drum. Somewhere within that cacophony of noise, Viper had fallen asleep.

Behind the dentist office lawn, a buckled concrete sidewalk ran perpendicular to the police car, disappearing behind a row of trees fringed with the verdant bloom of late springtime. Viper grunted.

Crawling through the window with his hands still cuffed proved more difficult than expected. He managed to slip his right leg through the window, supporting himself with his hands on the sill. As he dropped down upon his right leg, his left leg, still in the car, wedged up at a 90-degree angle. His nuts clipped the sill real good, and black spots clouded his vision. His groin flooding with agony, he fell sideways, and his left leg slipped through the window.

Free, Viper reassessed his situation. He no longer felt the effects of the Taser, but two prongs were stuck in his back. He should have run from the scene, but something told him that, crazy or not, nobody was coming to investigate the crash.

The underside of the police car was caught on a tree trunk leftover from a recent cutting. The front wheels were off the ground, spinning uselessly. Viper bent over, looking through the driver's window.

"You've got to be kidding me."

A key chain rested on the passenger seat where the fat cop had sat. Viper tried the handle and found the door unlocked. Slipping into the front seat, he pressed his foot down on the brake pedal and shifted the car into park. He snatched the key chain and sifted through about twenty keys until he found the one to unlock the cuffs. The locking mechanism sprang open.

"Thanks for doing me a solid, fatty. I owe you one."

Placing the cuffs on the passenger seat, he started to get out of the car. That's when he noticed the same pop country band was still on the radio, changing from one song to the next, as though an old school disc jockey had headed off to the john and left the CD to play unattended. He hit the scan button on the radio, hoping to find some Bible thumping zealot or maybe a death metal station as a parting gift for the kind officers who had given him a ride into town.

But the radio kept catching on stations transmitting static and cold silence. Knowing he was pushing his luck, Viper slipped out of the car, took one more look around to see that no one took notice of the accident, and walked toward a suburban neighborhood, looking as inconspicuous as a muscular bald dude who had just taken a joyride over a tree trunk could.

Walking into the late afternoon sun past ma and pa shops that formed a smallish town center, Viper noticed another curiosity. *All of the shops are empty.* Sure, it was common for small town businesses to close shop at 5 pm on Saturdays. But why did all of the signs on the doors say OPEN, and why were the lights on? Even if the shops were closed, there were bound to be a few people on the sidewalks. Another quandary. The town center was lined with vehicles, yet the streets were deserted.

To his right was a brick-faced antique shop set upon a perfectly manicured lawn of deep green. A quaint concrete pathway lined with purple and pink geraniums wound invitingly to the shop entrance. A white sign hanging over the pathway welcomed visitors to the *Exceptional Finds, the finest antiques in Brodus.* Viper had never heard of Brodus, Missouri, but he felt damn confident that it was a one-antique shop town. Like the other shops, a YES, WE'RE OPEN sign hung in the front door. The shop appeared as deserted as the others.

Half a block up the road, overcome by curiosity, he decided to check out Antonio's Pizza across the street. He looked both ways before crossing, but there wasn't so much as the hum of a distant motor. Birds chittered away in the trees. A black Labrador dog wandered out from behind the pizza place, tongue lolling. The dog barked once——a happy bark which said, *Hey, I sure am glad to see you*——and Viper extended an open hand. The dog padded forward, sniffed Viper's hand, and wagged his tail.

"Hey, boy. I'm new in town. Does this place serve

authentic Italian pizza, or is Antonio's real name Cletis?"

The dog cocked his head, whined, and padded back to where he had come from.

"That bad, eh? I guess I'll take my chances."

A red, neon sign in the window proclaimed Antonio's was open for business. The outer walls were green and red, and the scent of perfectly browned crust was on the wind. Mouth watering and stomach growling, Viper entered Antonio's.

Booths with green seat cushions lined the side walls. Round tables meant for two were scattered across the floor, though metal chairs were dragged to one table where four people had squeezed together for a meal. Upon two of the tables were large, uneaten pizzas. Full glasses of Cokes, beading with condensation that ran in rivulets across the tables, were set next to the plates.

"Hey. Anyone here?"

He stood listening to the deafening silence, knowing full well that nobody would answer. He strode to the metal counter. Behind the counter and to his left was a brick oven. Enclosed in glass beneath the counter was an assortment of red and green sweet peppers, long hot peppers, whole tomatoes and onions, homemade vinegars, and oils. The smells were intoxicating.

Turning away from the counter, he walked toward a table holding a thick crust pizza topped with sweet peppers and onions-—his favorite. He touched the crust. Still warm. He grabbed a slice and devoured it in five famished bites. He ate another slice, drank half a glass of Coke which was still cold, belched, and apologized to the missing guests for his bad manners. Then he grabbed a cardboard pizza box from a stack on the counter, threw the rest of the pizza in the box, and walked out the door.

The black lab was back, eying the pizza box in Viper's hand and drooling.

"Sorry, my friend. You aren't allowed to eat onions."

Viper opened the box and pulled off two handfuls of crust. "Here you go, pup." The dog took the crust in his mouth and ran off.

The sun lowered, and Viper's shadow elongated as it trailed him. He repeated the same procedure at three more shops——a mobile phone repair shop, a burger joint redolent of greasy fries, and a gas station mini mart. All were deserted, doors unlocked so anyone could take anything they wanted. *But there's nobody to take anything, is there?* Inside the mini mart, he ditched the pizza box, went behind the counter and made himself a 12-inch roast beef sub with all the fixings. He stuffed a dozen health food bars into his pockets.

Glancing up at the oval mirror in the corner, behind which was a security camera, he smiled and raised his middle finger. Half the state was probably looking for him for escaping from the police car—

No really, your honor. The officers waited until I was asleep, and then they jumped out of a moving vehicle and laughed their asses off while I bounced off a tree. Real funny bunch of officers you have in this here town of Brodus. They sure pulled a fast one on ole Viper, yessiree.

—so what difference did it make if he was caught on videotape filching a hoagie? Besides, times were about to get tough, and maybe he needed a little charity. You can't eat corn on the cob without teeth, and you can't make a living as a bounty hunter when there aren't any bad guys left to hunt.

Has the entire world vanished, or just Brodus? One thing was for sure: walking would get old, fast. So when he noticed the empty Highlander sitting beside the pumps with the keys still in the ignition, he accepted one more gift from Brodus.

He drove across miles of empty farmland with the bloody sun in his rear view mirror, past silos that stood like silent giants, weaving around the occasional shell of an abandoned automobile. Pressed against the road, fields of corn, sorghum, and wheat flourished without need for farmers and their machines.

Halfway to the Gateway Arch of St. Louis, the sun was a distant memory below the western horizon. A stranded vehicle rested on the shoulder every few tenths of a mile, gleaming in the starlight. Now and then he came upon a vehicle in the road, requiring him to jerk the Highlander's steering wheel to avoid a collision. A few of the vehicles still ran, their taillights glowing in the dusk. But nobody sat behind their wheels.

Viper's mouth went dry. He was alone in the world, and for the first time in his adult life, he had no goddamn idea what to do.

He did the only thing he could think to do. He kept driving, searching for signs of life in a dead world.

Ready for a wild ride? Grab your copy of Dark Vanishings on Amazon at http://www.amazon.com/dp/B00XGIE5O0 today!

The Island

Keep Reading!

Correspond directly with me. Each month I answer questions about my stories, give readers the scoop on my latest projects, review great books and movies, and run giveaways. Please join in on the fun by signing up at http://www.danpadavona.com/new-release-mailing-list/. You will only be contacted once or twice a month, and whenever a new book is about to be released. Your address will never be shared, and you can unsubscribe at any time.

If you liked Dark Vanishings, you'll LOVE my full-length, vampire horror novel, Storberry. Visit http://www.amazon.com/Storberry-Dan-Padavona-ebook/dp/B00N0D2LUG to start reading Storberry right now.

Storberry is an old-school thriller that returns the vampire mythos to its horrific roots. See what others are saying about Storberry:

"A Genuine Gem of the Horror Genre"

"A Classic Horror Novel"

"[Padavona's] descriptions paint vivid portraits in the mind and help with the visual 'Drive-In movie feel'."

"Finally a vampire story where the monsters are actually scary."

"Foreboding and moody. I love it!!!"

"[Padavona's] descriptive imagery is outstanding. I truly 'see' this town and the characters."

Ready to be scared? DOWNLOAD STORBERRY at

http://www.amazon.com/Storberry-Dan-Padavona-ebook/dp/B00N0D2LUG and turn the lights to low.

Author's Note

When I finished writing **Storberry**, I was genuinely pleased with the final product. However, I felt there was more to the vampire mythos that I wished to touch upon. The *human element* of vampirism was purposely avoided in **Storberry** to keep the monsters, well, monstrous.

In **One Autumn in Kane Grove**, we get to see the human side of the evil running amok through town without skimping on the horror. Kane Grove was a pleasure to write.

The Island was borne of a nightmarish vision of what might lurk in the uncharted corners of our world. Though I admit to finding spiders creepy, I rather like and certainly appreciate the little guys. Where would we be without them? Probably knee deep in mosquitoes.

Treman Mills is the darkest story I've written to date. I'm an unabashed fan of old school slasher horror and proto-slashers such as **The Texas Chainsaw Massacre**. Once I envisioned the abandoned building in rundown Treman Mills, the story quickly fell into place. The gore, while graphic and extreme, was a necessary element to keep the story as dark as I wanted it to be. I hope you enjoyed Treman Mills.

Thanks are once again in order for my wife Terri, and our children, Joe, and Julia. I also wish to thank the multitude of friends and family who have supported my efforts and become my first readers. You are my motivation, and I hope you continue to follow along on this exciting journey.

I wish to thank my editor, Jack Musci, who once again proved invaluable. Thank you for helping me track down the missing words and gremlins which seem always to elude the eye of the writer.

Although some of the locations surrounding the Lesser Antilles and Kane Grove are actual places, Kane

Grove itself, its university, and the lost island are wholly of the author's imagination. Any resemblance between the people in this book and people in the real world is purely coincidental and unintended.

About the Author

Dan Padavona is the author of the Dark Vanishings series, Storberry, Shadow Witch, and the horror anthology, The Island. He lives in upstate New York with his beautiful wife, Terri, and their children, Joe, and Julia. Dan is a meteorologist with NOAA's National Weather Service. Besides writing, he enjoys visiting amusement parks, beach vacations, Renaissance fairs, gardening, playing with the family dogs, and eating ice cream.

Visit Dan at: www.danpadavona.com

The Island

The Island

CPSIA information can be obtained
at www.ICGtesting.com
Printed in the USA
LVHW040308210723
753090LV00020B/192